ROT

The Day of Rot

RICHARD BESTEDER

ISBN 978-1-63961-267-3 (paperback)
ISBN 978-1-63961-268-0 (digital)

Copyright © 2023 by Richard Besteder

All rights reserved. No part of this publication may be reproduced, distributed, or transmitted in any form or by any means, including photocopying, recording, or other electronic or mechanical methods without the prior written permission of the publisher. For permission requests, solicit the publisher via the address below.

Christian Faith Publishing
832 Park Avenue
Meadville, PA 16335
www.christianfaithpublishing.com

Printed in the United States of America

Introduction

Rot, The Day of Rot, follows the book, *Red, The Saga of Red Dog*. The conclusion of the book of *Red* ends with some unfinished business. Rot, the son of Red, will take care of that business in a spectacular way that will be surprising and pleasing to the reader. The book of *Red* is incomplete without the book of *Rot*, and the book of *Rot* has no meaning unless you read the book on Red. Reading both books will help you to understand the relationships of both dogs and the humans related to both stories.

Rot, like Red, was a real dog. Much on Rot is true. But the sojourn of Rot and *The Day of Rot* is fiction. Many of the humans in the story of Rot are real people. The significance of Rot's story and what happens to people in it are exemplary of what happens in life. *Rot* is an excellent book because it is illustrated of good moral values. Also of note in Rot are various insights on the animal world of our Creator, always phenomenal.

The story of Rot, like that of Red, is told by a Watcher who chronicles for the Great King. There are Watchers among us (Daniel 4:17 NKJV). The King does not need chroniclers. He has books that contain records of every man and every woman's life—every thought, every feeling, every deed, everything (Revelation 20:12 NKJV). He knows every star, for He made it, and to each star, He has given a name (Psalm 147:4–5 NKJV). The King does not allow one sparrow to fall to the ground unless He wills for it to do so (Matthew 10:29 NKJV). The King owns every beast of the forest and all the birds of the mountains. He knows them, everyone (Psalm 50:10–11 NKJV). And what follows is *The Day of Rot*.

Chapter 1
The Wolf

The brick house was a new structure, the first on the left as one drove down a new street. There were two lanes divided by great oak trees growing in a ten-yard strip between the lanes. The first driveway, to the left, lined on each side by large oak trees, was a concrete entry, forty yards long. The house had two rows of large oaks in front of it and two on the backside. There were large oaks everywhere; the house sat in the middle. The two-anda-half-acre landscape included magnolia trees, dogwood trees, live oaks, hibiscus bushes, orange trees, palm trees, sego palms, and lots of azaleas. Lush dark green Augustine grass surrounded the house with assortments of bushes and floral arrangements everywhere. Visible from the main street was a large white three-decked fountain topped with kissing doves, out of which came a stream of running water at the left of the entryway into the house.

Well, thought Jake who was a little low on cash, *this looks like a place where I can pick up some funds or items I can trade at one of our local pawnshops.* Jake the Rake, as they called him, turned his county truck to the left, going through the passageway in the street's divide, and started up the roadway to the brick house. No cars were in the driveway.

His cover was perfect. He was looking for a stray red dog someone had reported in this area. It was always the red dog. He picked up his hatred for the red dog from his friend, Fitz. If someone were home, Jake would give them a story and come back later with the same mission. Jake was going to get into this house, and he was sure it would be rewarding.

Parking his truck in front of the three-car garage, he followed the sidewalk around to the east side of the house, pausing to look at the kissing doves on top of the water fountain, and then down past the blooming hibiscus on his right, to the large double doors in front of him. The doors were oak with large windows. Rake did not ring the doorbell, but cupping his right hand on his forehead above his eyes, he leaned forward, straining to see what was inside.

Jake, who had already looked to his right through a window into the dining room, had seen on top of a serving table a large pewter punch bowl, cups, and various settings. "This is going to be good," Jake murmured to himself. But there was something standing off to the side of the window, inside the dining room, against the wall that the Rake did not see.

Looking into the great room, Jake saw a tile floor with a decorative designed entryway, leather chairs, off to the left, a large fireplace with bookshelves on each side, and still further to the left, a large wall-mounted flat-screen television. But now something was obscuring his vision. The room, well-lit by large glass doors on the room's opposite side, was slowly becoming black, pitch-black. The black seemed to slide from the dining room right, along the entry inside the great doors, until it appeared directly in front of Jake, peering at him as he stood peering into the house.

Jake knew he was slow. Focusing, he stiffened and then began to shake. There, staring right back at him, was a huge beast. It was, yes, a giant dog. Jake should be able to identify a dog. After all, catching dogs was his business. Jake would later swear this dog had a head like a lion. Its neck was like a tree trunk. Its eyes gleamed red. The dog's ears laid back, its long tail forked stiffly up, the hair on its back stood ridged, and its lips were raised, revealing gleaming white incisors. All of this could be seen with various German shepherds, Doberman pinschers, or rottweilers. But this dog was different. Even on the other side of the door—his mien was scary. It was the way he looked at you, his piercing glare, frightening, penetrating eyes. It was his body posture, his aggressive stance, a surreal ferocious wild beast from a primitive forest—stalking forward, about to pounce upon you. It was his intensity, the utter confidence that he was going to dispense you and that right quickly. It was his muscles, rippling giant limbs.

He must have been all of two hundred pounds.

Rake, of course, wanted no part of this animal. He could only think of one word—WOLF. And Jake said it. It was like involuntarily. It just came out like an explosion of gas, only out of his vocal cords. Out it whisked—"WOLF."

This, of course, was Rot's territory. His vocation was a guard dog. He was told to protect the house. He took pride in what he did. And Rake had done the one thing that someone in Rot's area must not do—he looked directly into Rot's eyes. This was a challenge. And it was accepted. Rot burst forward—thumping against the door with a great bang. The door shook. Rot stood as high as Jake the Rake. A snarling growl seeped through his lips, and his head twisted from side to side. It looked like he was coming right through the door.

It took Jake a second to break out of his paralysis. Jake did an about-face. Fleeing down the sidewalk, he dived into his truck, leaving a patch of rubber in reverse and forward as he sped down and out of the driveway.

Soiled and now angry but unashamed, the villain that he was, Jake stopped two miles down the road at a bar he frequented to drown his frustration. Lo and behold, who was there but his buddy, Fitz. "Fitz!" Jake exclaimed as he slid on a barroom stool, to the right of his partner in underhanded activities. "Fitz, I just saw the most horrible dog that ever lived. I'm lucky to be alive."

Fitz, a beer in his right hand, elevated halfway to his slobbery lips, lackadaisically moved his head toward Jake, and shifted his eyes like he was just coming out of a trance. "Hum," muttered Fitz.

The Rake let loose a bombastic string of verbiage, interspersed with profanity, complaining how hard it was these days to carry out an honest heist. Going into a detailed description of the wolf quartered in a nearby house that surely contained a veritable treasure of goodies, Jake railed about how unfair it was that he could not get what should be his.

Fitz, who had been listening as though half dazed, with an "uh" and "ah" here and there, sleepily remarked, "I don't see the problem." Fitz was a man of great talent at pilfering, cruelty, and deception. He was a natural leader when it came to anything criminal. It was not necessary for him to engage in deep thought. Fitz, being the authority that he was, pontificated, "Get a steak, put some strychnine on it, break open the window nearest the door handle, and throw the steak through the hole in the broken window to the dog."

"But," said Jake, "suppose the dog doesn't eat the steak?"

"It will," replied Fitz. "Dogs are dumb animals. They go by instinct and do not think or reason. This dog will be like every other. Its desire will be for the meat—meat, did you hear me, boy? The meat. Get the meat. The dog will forget all about you. Go about your business, and the dog will be dead."

Jake uttered, "Meat, yes, the meat. Yes, the meat. Dogs will always go for meat. Even I would go for the meat. What about the strychnine? Do we have any left?"

"There's some in my truck," muttered Fitz. "You know where it is. Use it."

In less than an hour, Jake was back at the brick house. Rot, barking and growling, was bouncing off the entryway doors. "Ah," said the Rake, boisterously, "I have something for you, mighty dog." With the authority of Fitz, undaunted, Jake smashed his ball-peen hammer through the window of the right door adjacent to the door handle. With three well-aimed blows, he opened an appropriate-sized hole through which he could shove the poison steak, after which he would insert his hand and open the door from the inside.

Jake inserted the steak through the hole and gave it a push. Confident that the wolf dog would go for the steak, thin, six-foot-three, Rake, quickly stuck his right hand through the broken window to unlatch the door lock and open the front right door.

Rot, however, completely oblivious to the steak, instantly grabbed unto Jake's right hand. Jake yanked forward, cutting his wrist and arm on the broken window. Like a squirrel in the clutches of a great hawk, Jake froze, making no resistance or uttering a sound. Then, an amazing thing happened. Rot let loose. Jake withdrew his bleeding arm, followed by a somewhat emasculated hand. Once again, down the sidewalk, he trekked. Using his left hand, he got into his van and left, all the while cursing Fritz as he went slowly on his way to the emergency at the nearby local hospital.

Chapter 2

Cry of the Hawks

The oak doors swung open, and out stepped Preacher, accompanied by Rot. They walked past the kissing doves, turned left, down the sidewalk to the drive, beginning their morning constitutional.

Shrill cries filled the morning air—*kheeeea, kheeeea, kheeeea*, sounded Dog Hawk as he left his perch in the large oak from where he had been expectantly watching the twin oak doors. He flew to the east, overhead the drive being traversed by Rot. Three other hawks, one his mate, and two others, his young hawks, all having been in oak trees to the north of the house, took to the air, speeding parallel to the road the Preacher and Rot would stroll. *Kheeeea, kheeeea, kheeeea*, they cried a threefold announcement to the squirrels, crows, hidden turkeys, or anything else that was about. "It's him, it's him, it's him." North, over the twin lanes they flew, and on they went, followed by Dog Hawk, who was again, screeching, *kheeeea, kheeeea, kheeeea*. Sometimes, they would perch in oaks and watch Rot. Other times, they flew speeding on to their morning haunts.

The hawks were there many mornings. Rot was oblivious to them. *Oblivious* is a good word. It is a good word because Rot knew the hawks were there, and he knew what it was about. If anything described Rot, it was awareness. Like his mother, Red, he always knew what was about and what it was about. Rot missed nothing. But to observe Rot, you would never know that he knew.

It is like that with the creation, especially these days. Mankind is not in touch with his environment. A person would not know the hawks were there or why they cried as they did. But Preacher knew. Sometimes he would say, "It's Dog Hawk and his brood." And that was all. Other times, he said nothing. And like Rot, he, too, seemed oblivious to the hawks.

When the hawks watched Rot, school was in session. Rot had a peculiar saunter. His back legs moved like that of a Rot, a pigeon-toed canter, a dog pugilist that sounded a bell for the hawks—danger, danger, danger. Yet the redbone mix in him, the hound variation, lent to Rot sniffing like a bloodhound, every scent on the roadway and along it on plants and trees. Rot read it all like a morning devotional, knowing what had transpired since his walk the night before. And the wolf in Rot kept his head high, searching, looking ahead, twisting from side to side, and pausing often to look back, noting every detail of the landscape, close-up, and in the distance for a hundred yards and beyond. It would be virtually impossible to sneak up on this dog. Rot's nostrils were forever moving, testing every scent in the air. And thanks to Dog Hawk, Rot, unlike most dogs, constantly accessed what might be coming from above.

Dog Hawk was obsessed with Rot. He was in awe of Rot yet hated him. Since he snatched the puppy in his talons, and the dog, twisting and turning, had caused him to smash into a tree, thus losing the dog as prey, also doing considerable damage to his body as well as his ego, he had watched with addicting interest the dog as he grew. Now Rot lived in a different location, not far as a hawk flies, only a few miles from their original battle. Dog Hawk had relocated Rot. Dog Hawk and his brood vigilantly monitored Rot, hoping for an opportunity to inflict vengeful pain.

Rot had only been six weeks old when he had come to the top of the burrow of his birth to sit at its entrance and look at his newfound world. His mother, Red dog, was away. Dog Hawk, who had spied Rot outside his lair earlier, had found a perch from which he could spring to snatch away the little black-haired steak. Rot's great-grandfather, on his mother's side, was the great white wolf, so Rot was exceptionally inbred for survival. As Dog Hawk descended, Rot's peripheral vision picked up his movement. Though a pup, Rot shuffled, moving to his right. Instead of snatching the pup dead center, Dog Hawk latched onto the rear part of Rot's back. With an unbalanced catch, twisting and turning, resisting, struggling Rot threw Dog Hawk into a spin. Dog Hawk hit an oak tree and unconsciously fell to the ground. Meanwhile, Rot, thrown further beyond, landed on a bank with his back torn and bleeding.

Dog Hawk, coming to consciousness, dizzily flew off, unable for the moment to remember what had happened. Later, he was incensed. No dog had ever escaped his prowess. Dog Hawk's visage was so terrifying that animals froze while he ate them alive. His rate of success was 100 percent. Dog Hawk clearly understood these factors, and what had happened with Rot continually gnawed at him. What Dog Hawk could not comprehend was how the little dog got away. Therefore, Dog Hawk's attention was fixated on Rot.

Preacher had been mowing the lawn near where Rot had fallen two days before. He kept hearing a cry but could not recognize what it was. His wife, Elaine, later told him she heard the same cry when she went to work that morning. Finishing his mowing, Preacher went to investigate. The sound led him to a bank off to the east of his house. Straining his eyes, he saw something white and black. Preacher uttered, "It's a puppy." Walking forward, he reached down and picked it up. As the crying puppy was raised from the ground, it twisted its head, and its eyes looked into the face of Preacher, into the eyes of its rescuer. It was a moment Preacher would never forget. It was a moment Rot would never forget. It was a moment of bonding. It was the master and the saved.

Rot was dying. The white on Rot were maggots eating where his back had been ripped open by the talons of Dog Hawk. The puppy was covered with fleas. He needed water and food. If Preacher had not come along, Rot would have expired that very day. The Bible often speaks of prayer as crying out to God. Note in Joel 1:20, "The beasts of the field who do not have water cry out to God." Animals cry out. The puppy, later called Rot, cried out. He was heard and saved.

Preacher took Rot home and cleaned him up. Rot was taken to a vet in DeLand. He was cleaned up, given shots, and put on the road to health. The damage done by Dog Hawk was so great that it could not be repaired. To this day, Rot carries a hairless mark on his back in the shape of Dog Hawk.

The vet said Rot was a rottweiler. Thus, Preacher called him "Rot." Preacher knew he was sired by Red the redbone who had been pregnant and had built a burrow nearby. In fact, now Preacher understood what Red had been doing some time earlier when she had showed up behind his house. She had been looking for a place to birth her pups. The vet, also examining Rot's feet, said, "Look at this dog's feet. It is going to be a large dog."

Chapter 3

Home Sweet Home

Rot had what every dog ought to have and Red never had, and that is a permanent home. Rot now had, in the earlier part of his life, security. A dog knows when he or she is loved. One of the saddest experiences one can have is to walk through a dog shelter and look into the eyes of the caged canines, eyes of fear, eyes that know they are in deep trouble, about to be put to sleep for the absence of someone who will take them home, eyes that plead, "Take me, take me," eyes that cry help. The eyes may not know what they are saying, but they are pleading, "Please adopt me—please."

When Preacher first found Rot in his pitiful condition, he was deeply emotionally touched. Picking up the injured dying pup, he held its tiny head in front of his face, looked into its eyes, and said, "Little dog, don't be afraid. I will take care of you all the days of your life. You will always have a home, and you will always have the best."

When the preacher returned from the vet, his wife was home from work. She reminded him they had agreed, after the death of the last dog, "Lady," a miniature schnauzer, that they would not have any more dogs. "But," said Preacher, "this pup is special. He is a gift from God. I promised to keep him and to take care of him all the days of his life."

Elaine, his wife, reluctantly agreed.

Discussing Rot with Elaine, Preacher said, "Evidently, this is a pup of the Red dog, the redbone, we saw wandering around behind our house some weeks ago. I wonder what happened to her?

Tomorrow, I'm going to look around and see if there are any more pups."

The next day, on a bank in the wooded area behind their small backyard, about twenty-five yards from the house, Preacher discovered a burrow. The entrance was some two feet above ground level, about ten feet deep, slanting upward, so water would not get into Red dog's den. It had been raining for weeks, hard downpours day after day, but Red's lair was dry. The typical wolf excavation is strategically located and laboriously dug. Red dog's absence meant she must have run into some difficulty. She was alone and had no pack for support. Preacher knew it would be best to rescue any pups he found on the premise.

Sitting on top of the burrow were two pups, one a black female that had markings like Rot's, and another a large male that was totally white. Preacher scooped them up and took them home.

Both dogs were taken to Rot's newfound vet. All three were quartered in the large laundry room, adjacent to the kitchen in the house Preacher was renting. The large white pup was evidently an alpha dog, for he would not roll on his back, thus exposing his under section. Nevertheless, in play, he was dominated by Rot.

Preacher referenced the dogs in a message to the congregation where he ministered. The white male puppy and black female puppy were adopted by church families.

Rot continued to live in the laundry room in the evening, while he roamed around the house most of the day. Often his was in the master bedroom with Preacher and Elaine, sometimes until late at night. His favorite activity was running up and down the steps between the first and second floors. In the beginning, he would jump a step at a time. Being quite small, and his size increasing, he would skip steps leaping over multiple ones in a mad gallop to the top or a flight downward to the first floor.

Midway down the steps, Rot liked to sit on a landing, looking over the living room below or out the great windows off the stairway over the front lawn and bank to the road below. From the beginning, he was interested in all traffic: cars, people walking their dogs, or whatever was transpiring outside the house.

The staircase was bordered by a wall on the left and a rail to the right with wood slats running from it, connecting to the stair frame. While Rot sat on the landing, Preacher would approach the landing from the room below and stick a hand between one of the slats to grab him. It was a friendly game of "got you." Rot quickly developed strategies to ward off Preacher's attacks. Preacher began to use both hands, feigning a grab here or there, using one hand to attempt a grab but quickly shifting to the other for a quick catch. Rot learned quickly, so he pretty much knew from any movement what Preacher was going to do. He evaded Preacher's best attempts to get him and speedily grabbed Preacher's hand with a playful nip. Preacher observed; Rot is not an ordinary dog. He is highly intelligent, amazing quick, and he conceptualizes, thinking up clever ways of whatever is necessary to cope with what is confronting him. Rot had the cunning, even as a pup, of a great alpha wolf.

As he grew, and people would come by to visit, Preacher would put him in the upstairs master bedroom with the door closed. In short order, there would be Rot, sitting quietly in the living room, listening to the conversation. Preacher was telling Rot's vet about it. He said, "Over and over, I would shut Rot up in our master bedroom, and there he would be, by my side in the house. Each time, I was sure I had shut the door with him in the bedroom. Until one day, I stood outside the door and watched. Rot was opening the door from the inside and coming down the steps."

The vet was explaining to me that such was not uncommon with the handle-type door openers I had in my rented house. Then I said to the vet, "Look, he is standing on his hind legs, using his front paws, attempting to turn your doorknob and open the door."

The vet commented, "That is one smart dog."

From the beginning, as a puppy and all through his life, Rot would sit in his favorite leather recliner and stare at Preacher or whoever was in the living room. He watched and listened, observed and thought. Sometimes, he would twist his head—seriously pondering the meaning of what he was witnessing and how to process it. He did the same wherever he was, like outside in the yard with animals and people as they moved about in the neighborhood.

ROT

It was a joy to be with Rot. Sometimes, Preacher, sitting in the living room would notice Rot was focused steadfastly on him, observing his every word and action. When Preacher stared back, after a few minutes, Rot would look away. When Preacher looked away and then he looked back, he would discover Rot was staring at him once again. Rot was a thinker—a thinking dog. He was always thinking.

Chapter 4
Dog Karate

After Preacher found Rot and accepted him into his family in the house that he and his wife rented, Preacher would take Rot outside, walking and running around their yard. The paved driveway running from the garage had a steep incline for some fifty feet south and then made a sharp turn west, inclining downward to the Black Ironwood Drive. A quart plastic container had fallen from the large house trash can and was at the top of the drive. Preacher was at the bottom of the incline, looking up at Rot who was playfully chiding him. Rot picked up the container with his jaws and darted down the drive, trying to get it past Preacher. Preacher tried to intercept him and take the container from his grasp. This activity developed into a game.

Rot was the one who initiated this fun exercise. Together, Preacher and Rot developed it into a contest. No one kept score, but Preacher, intercepting the empty plastic container, would try to kick it back up the driveway and to the place where Rot first picked it up. Rot would attempt to counter his move by snatching the container, carrying it down the driveway to the grass off the pavement, dropping it there, a little past where the driveway curved to the west. To score, Rot had to get by Preacher with the container. Preacher had been a sprinter in high school track. Even though that was some years ago, he still moved quite fast. He had also played linebacker in high school football, having developed quick deceptive moves as well as the skill to make the final move for a successful tackle, or in this case, to grab hold of Rot or wrench the plastic container from his jaws.

Sometimes, there would be a tug of war with the container. Preacher was amazed at Rot's speed, even as a maturing young dog. He was also impressed at Rot's ability to stop or slow up, feign a move this way or that to avoid capture and to triumphantly get the container by Preacher for a score. The two spent many pleasurable hours with this activity.

This game was followed by another more significant enterprise. Preacher bought a dog toy, a hard rubber device shaped like a loped rope on both ends with a rubber piece connecting the middle. Rot would latch onto one end with his teeth, and Preacher would hold fast to the other end, pulling with either his left or right hand. Rot, of course, grew into a dog well over a hundred pounds. Preacher, six-foot-one and 220 pounds, early in this enterprise, was able to lift Rot into the air with one hand. A gargantuan struggle between Rot and Preacher regularly occurred as they competed for dominance. It was something an alpha wolf would enjoy. Rot wanted to so engage every day.

Somehow this developed into a sport that Preacher called "Dog Karate." Preacher would swing his right or left foot to thump Rot on his right or left shoulder, not hard but playfully. Rot quickly learned to move in the appropriate direction to avoid Preacher's contact. The game got quicker and quicker. Soon, Preacher, no matter how swift he moved, could not touch Rot. As this sport developed, Preacher would sweep his right or left foot under Rot's right or left front leg, attempting to knock Rot down, thus making him let loose of his end of the loped toy. Rot caught on to this tactic, and again, Preacher could not touch him. Rot eventually grew to be 125 pounds. He was more than a match for Preacher.

From the beginning, Rot had quickly conceptualized how to counter any attack Preacher could devise to best him. And these daily workouts meant anyone who tried to kick or hit Rot was engaging in a useless endeavor. Rot learned to quickly move to the right or to the left or hastily step back, whichever was required to avoid a fast-swiping foot or to evade a kick or hit of any kind.

Preacher, using different moves for deception in the beginning of Dog Karate, used moves to the right or left and a quick thrust of either foot to sweep one of Rot's back legs out from under him. For the first few times, Preacher, moving exceedingly fast, faking a front leg kick on one side but delivered a kick under Rot's rear leg on the other. It worked once but then never again. Preacher then would attempt to use his right or left hand to thumb Rot on the right or left shoulder to make him let loose of the toy, and finally, alongside of his head to reflect a release.

In all this, Rot became highly skilled like a person highly trained in martial arts, instantly recognizing from Preacher's movement any forthcoming yank, a swinging hand or foot, whatever was coming his way with any kind of a body movement. Whatever was attempted did not work, for wherever you struck, Rot was no longer there. It became impossible to touch Rot in combat, for he became exceedingly proficient in developing coping evasive counter measures for every contingency. Thus, Preacher worked with Rot, preparing him—always preparing him. For what? He did not know. If ever there was such a thing as a black belt in Dog Karate, Rot was worthy of it.

Like Rot's mother, Red, who played with her friend, Sandy, many games of hide-and-seek and such, Sandy always being outwitted, Rot, too, had the cunning DNA of the great white wolf. It should be noted in these contests, while it was impossible to touch Rot, he did not run away. Sandy, in their games, would think Red ran away, but she was mistaken. Red used the tactic of a wolf to deceive, and when you thought she was gone, Sandy would be surprised to find Red right behind her, nudging one of her legs. Red purposively led you to think she was vulnerable, turning it into an advantage for herself.

Though you could not touch Rot, and he might retreat a step or two, he was still there. Later, in his new home, he might run off in the great room, toward the kitchen because he knew he could turn right circle through the panty room, into the dining room, and come up behind you, according to where you had been engaging in combat in the great room.

All this, of course, was play for Rot. He enjoyed it, and for him, it was a daily workout, a fun time to relate to a member of his pack, the one who had rescued him, saved him. He was bonded to Preacher, and the bond was strengthened day by day. Preacher, too, thrived on this activity because it gave him a good workout and his affection continued to build for what he considered to be a great dog. Most days, when Preacher came home from work, Rot would go to his box of personal items, remove the double loop ended toy, bringing it to Preacher, holding out an end of it for Preacher, communicating, "Let's go at it."

And they would go at it—Dog Karate—all over the house and all over the front and backyard, alongside the house, in the driveway, and later, in Preacher's new house, on two-and-a-half acres, all over the yard, woods, and front field. They roughed it.

Chapter 5

Best Buddies

The best photo of Preacher and Rot is when Rot was just a few months old, and Preacher was sitting halfway up the bottom steps to the second story of his rented house. Rot was on the step behind Preacher, standing on his hind legs with his front paws, one on Preacher's right shoulder and the other on his left. Rot was looking intensely over Preacher at the camera. He was photogenic and true to his nature, always stared intelligently at the camera when photos were taken. Preacher loved the photo because it communicated from Rot, "We are best buddies." And of course, they were, always.

Wherever Preacher was in the house, there was Rot, lying by his side or at Preacher's feet before the chair in which he sat. Outside, Rot walked beside Preacher. When in Preacher's red JC7 Jeep, purchased through the air force AFFES system when he was a USAF Chaplain in South Dakota, Rot sat in the passenger seat, and if Elaine, Preacher's wife, was present, Rot sat in the back seat with his front paws on the console and his head between the two. He loved to ride standing on his hind feet with his front feet on the window frame and his head hanging out the window, air blowing in his face, as he took in the passing landscape, including many dogs and all kinds of people. He was a watcher and missed nothing.

At first, during the night, Rot was confined to the laundry room, but somehow, Preacher's memory fails here. Rot began to sleep beside the bed in their master bedroom, and then somehow or other, he got promoted to the middle of their king-sized bed. If he got too close to either Preacher or Preacher's wife, Elaine, he had to leave the bed and sleep on the carpet beside Preacher's side of the bed. He soon learned how to sleep without making it inconvenient for either Preacher or his wife.

Early on, when Rot was still a pup, Preacher took Rot to a church picnic at Blue Springs Park in Orange City. Rot enjoyed watching the manatees, all the various types of people, and an assortment of other dogs. Preacher was approached by three different people who asked questions about Rot and wanted to purchase him. He was kept on a leash in compliance with the park rules and other people who had to do so with their dogs.

A church member had a mature, belligerent Chihuahua that tried to bite Rot. Though yet a small dog but already in dog karate, when the Chihuahua snapped its jaws shut to grab his right hind leg, Rot was no longer there. Rot, true to his temperament, bit the Chihuahua on the nose. There was a great deal of howling, and Mr. Chihuahua made sure for the rest of the picnic that he kept far away from Rot. It would be Rot's character not to bother other dogs, but if attacked, the other dog learned never to do it again.

The church where Preacher pastored, the Garden, was only a of couple miles away from where he rented, so he would often take Rot there and let him run loose on the thirteen-acre grounds. Rot enjoyed running beneath the great oaks and smelling the many assortments of flowers and flowery bushes. Inside the main building, he wandered around, harming nothing, and most of the time, he would lie beside Preacher's chair at the desk while Preacher worked on a sermon or some project.

On Sunday nights, he accompanied Preacher and Elaine to church, lying in the center isle between the chairs, listening intently, his eyes focused on Preacher as his mother, Red, had done some years earlier, listening to the community's pastor. Preacher always believed Rot understood more than church people imagined. There were many dog lovers present, and all seemed to readily accept Rot, mostly amused by his presence and surprised by his demeanor.

Early on, Rot's intelligence and cunning were observed by Preacher, one day, by an incidence in front of their rented house.

Preacher was sitting on the lawn bank in front of the house with Rot at his right side. They were observing birds, dogs, cars, and whatever was traveling down Black Ironwood, the street in front of their house. Along came a young muscular athletic man dressed in a T-shirt, shorts, running shoes, and a baseball-type cap, pedaling an expensive bike. Riding east, he looked to be holding about a seven-foot leash in his right hand, the one toward the side of the road where Preacher and Rot sat. Running alongside him was a large brown shepherd, a big fella. Rot jumped up and started barking. His bark was somewhat shrill, since he was still a pup only about four months old. The shepherd broke loose from its owner and charged up the bank of the lawn after Rot.

Rot, of course, was no longer there. In an instant, he sprinted for his house, went through the open front doorway with the shepherd close behind. Bouncing through the living room, he hooked right, racing up the stairs to the first flight. The shepherd halted, hesitating, and was totally shocked when he saw Rot in a giant leap, sailing through the air, all four legs stretched out like a flying squirrel. Rot impacted the much larger dog like a skilled linebacker sacking the opposing quarterback with a tremendous thud that sent the pursuing shepherd flat on the living room floor.

Before the shepherd could recover, his owner was there, grabbing his dog's leash, vociferously apologizing. As he quickly led his dog away and resumed his ride, there was, from ear to ear, a large smirk on Rot's face. In future days, Preacher and Rot would watch the duo traverse by, and the bike rider would wave, while the large shepherd had a smirk of his own, like "You are okay, pup." Preacher would wave, and Rot would look at Preacher, the wave, the rider, and return wave, and always, there was the smirk.

Chapter 6
The Feral Dog

Between their karate, competitive games, walks, and other activities, Preacher and Rot would sit in the grass, the lawn, on the south side of their rented house facing a vacant lot, empty field, near where Preacher found Rot. Rot would stare at the uncut high grass in fixation, giving it his total attention. Preacher, raised in a mountainous area of Eastern Pennsylvania and acquainted with wildlife, knew there was something present. In fact, it was Rot's mother, Red, always near, yet unseen.

    Preacher walked Rot every day, up Black Ironwood south, left down the main road, turning left at the next street, then left and left, back to his home street, and their house. It was his practice to read late and then to walk Rot in the dark with a .357 Colt Python in his belt, in front of his stomach, and a flashlight in his left hand. Rot would be on a leash he held in his right hand, and since Preacher had grown up traversing the forest after dark, sometimes hunting raccoons, he had learned to use the light sparingly. Once one's eyes adjusted to the dark, you learned how not to use your flashlight, for it in fact blinded you to everything out there not in the beam's direct path. Nights when there was a full moon, you could see quite well.

    It had been hot that day, and in the cool of the evening, there was a dense fog. As Preacher and Rot were halfway through the fourth leg of their evening constitution, off to the right, about ten yards ahead, a large form emerged. Preacher stopped. He could see it was a huge dog. Then to its right, on the other side of this apparition silently emerged another large dog, and then another. So here was a pack of feral dogs. Then a fourth dog appeared out of the midst. It walked slowly past the others, directly toward Preacher and Rot. Stopping about ten feet in front of Rot, it stood quietly, staring intensely at him. Preacher recognized Red. Rot moved to the end of his leash, staring back, sniffing but making no sound, not a whine or whimper. For some minutes, they stood. Then Red turned, walking back past her pact, disappearing off to the right from whence she had come, into the night as mysteriously as she had appeared. Her pact, having made no sound, turned and followed her.

Preacher noted that folk who had bought puppies often abandoned them when they were full-grown. They would drop their dog off in this well-to-do neighborhood, thinking people with money would have compassion on a stray dog and adopt it. This, of course, was a very cruel thing to do to a dog. Just the opposite of what some people supposed was how it really was. People who had beautiful yards did not want a stray dog rooting around in it. They would be the first to call animal control to have the dog removed. People who had less means were more apt to have two or three dogs and more readily to adopt another.

Domesticated dogs loved as adorable puppies and raised in a home environment could not comprehend why their owner would one day just take them for a ride and put them out of their car or truck and leave them. They did not know what to do, how to cope or to survive. Preacher would see them running or lying along the roadway, frightened, and dismayed. They often got run over by a car, or in some cases, folks who despised what had become a feral dog would shoot them. It was such dogs as these that Red had adopted and now constituted her pack. They followed her because she knew what to do. They were desperate, and Red was an alpha.

For the most part, no one saw Red. But a few in the neighborhood at one time or another saw the large dogs in the forested areas around where they lived. Animal control was called in and, one by one, these dogs were caught and hauled off for extermination. Red, however, was never caught because she was too intelligent to go into a cage with food in it and past a trapdoor that would spring shut once a dog was inside.

There was a kindhearted widow that lived in a large house with its backyard bordering on the forested area where Red had come to hunt. Red would come out in the evening, just before dust, and the woman would feed her and set out a large pan of water for her. Red trusted her, but even so, would not allow the woman to touch her and maintained a distance of at least twenty feet away. Preacher knew about this situation and had become a friend of the widow. With her permission, he would take Rot to her backyard, and Rot would visit his mother.

Red only touched noses with him a couple of times and always remained aloft. Preacher would talk to Red, and sometimes, she would do a little jig for him, a special little dance. It of course meant it was a joy for her to have Preacher and Rot there. Preacher was glad there was some happiness in her life. He would call her, trying to get her to come so he could get a leash on her and find her a home. Something or someone had badly hurt her, thus she would not allow anyone to touch her and always stayed about ten feet away. Every time Preacher visited, it seemed Red trusted him more, and he hoped the day would come when Red would no longer be feral.

A neighbor whose house was next to the widow had witnessed animal control haul away a couple of the large dogs in Red's pack. Preacher went over on one of these occasions to talk to the animal control guys. The one in charge, the fat, short one, identified himself as Fritz. The tall skinny one said his name was Jake. The neighbor who lived next to the widow was telling Fritz that a red dog was the leader of these vicious wild dogs. Fritz brought his right hand up to his chin, and like the famous statue of the Thinker, became engrossed in deep thought. "A red dog," he murmured. "The red dog. Hum!"

The neighbor, with a north easterner city brogue, was bragging about having a rifle, a twenty-two, and promising to shoot the red dog. Preacher gave him a long contemptuous stare. Turning his back on him, he asked Fritz from whence he hailed. Not answering, Fritz asked Preacher the same question. Preacher replied, "A little town in North Eastern Pennsylvania. Its name means love dogs."

Fritz gulped. He made a short gasp for air. "I've got to go," he stammered. Fritz promptly got into his animal control truck. Jake got in on the other side, and they were gone.

Chapter 7

Rot's Territory

Preacher and his wife, Elaine, were having a new house constructed in a wooded area, off Glenwood Road, just a few miles from their rented house. It was on a two-and-a-half-acre lot, the first to be built in that area. Almost daily, they would ride over in their red Jeep, top off, with Rot only a few months old, sitting obediently in the back seat, enjoying the fresh Florida country air, and the wind blowing in his face.

While the leading members of his pack walked around, inspecting this or that relating to the new house being constructed, Rot would roam the territory, investigating the new grounds over which he would be guard dog. Rot would earn his keep. He would come to know that he had purpose, and he would take his work seriously. This land was his land, and in the coming days and years, it would be abundantly clear that it was his territory. Any person or animal that stepped foot on his property would know immediately that this was Rot land, and no funny business would be tolerated.

Because of Rot's size and demeanor, Rot was always the center of attention when anyone came up the fifty-yard concrete drive between the rows of giant oaks on each side. If anyone looked inside the large glass front doors, and no one was present, intruders left rather quickly. UPS and FEDEX delivery people learned never to go around the side of the house, up the sidewalk, to the front door to deliver packages. They left whatever they were delivering under the overhang of the roof in front of the three-car garage, the first part of the house accessible from the drive.

The comments were always the same: "Did you see that dog?"

"Yea, if that dog wanted, the dog could come right through those doors."

Snoopers walking around the housing area who came up the drive, past the garage and looked left, into the large brown wood framed windows, into the kitchen nook, or the large twin sliding glass doors in the back, the west side of the house, would see Rot once and depart hastily, never to return. Rot, of course, would put on a little warning performance, lifting his lips, revealing his large white teeth, uttering a guttural growl, his long tail pointing straight up, the hair on the back of his neck standing, and taking a few steps forward, putting his giant front feet on the door or window standing from inside to a height above a six-foot-three man. No one had any doubt that he could back up his threat, "Don't come in here or try to come in here while my folks are away. Come into my domain, and you will really be sorry."

In the early months of his life, Rot ran hither and thither around the trees and building material for the new house, sniffing everything. The redbone hound in him, partly inherited from the bloodhound, always exploring, learning to identify by scent every sort of animal or life that was present or had been in the recent hours or days before. In the back of his mind, Rot understood there was a matter of some unfinished business to which he was inwardly driven. Little did he know that he was being prepared for a great trial that would unfold later in the days to come.

The outside of Preacher's house on all four sides was completely styled from the ground to the roof with light brownish red attractive bricks. Underneath the bricks, laid first, were concrete blocks. Prior to the concrete blocks being used, they sat on the property in long rows about waist-high to Preacher. Each block laid faceup, having three oval shaped holes in it. A game Preacher played with Rot was to place him on the block pile at one end and have him run to Elaine at the other end of the pile. It was hard to do so because puppy Rot's feet kept slipping into the block holes. Preacher would walk alongside Rot to see that he did not get hurt. When one of Rot's feet would slip into a hole, Preacher would lift him up and put him once again on top of the blocks. In this fun activity, Rot learned to navigate across the block pile with never slipping into one of the blocks holes. It was quite a feat. Rot acquired the skill of running across the blocks without slipping into a hole.

So as Elaine called Rot, and he came to her, learning to walk across the blocks, avoiding the holes. He stepped in such a way as to walk on the edge of the blocks and holes without falling into a hole. Rot became so good at it that, soon, he could run across the blocks. In his mind, he associated the blocks with the holes and what would happen if a dog tried to run across the blocks and did not know what he was doing. Rot, a super intelligent dog with a wolf's instinct, evidently processed all this information in his mind and filed it away for any use he might have for it in the future.

Rot with Preacher visited this construction day by day, inspecting it and monitoring the progress. Toward the completion of their new dwelling, Preacher went up a ladder placed against the back side of the large single-level house to look at the newly laid blue shingle roof. Standing on the new elevation, Preacher, with great satisfaction, looked in all directions, scanning the surrounding majestic trees and forested acreage of other lots, which were soon to have an assortment of beautiful new houses. Preacher, hearing a scraping noise behind him, slowly turned and, to his surprise, there was Rot, gingerly making his way off the top of the ladder, onto the newly laid roof. Preacher, chuckling, squatted down, gesturing for Rot to come forward, for a good pet and belly rub. Preacher, looking directly into Rot's eyes, his left hand holding his chin up so his face was only a foot or so away, uttered, "You little, daredevil. You never cease to amaze me."

Together they walked around the roof for some minutes, Rot taking in the ground over which he was soon to be the master.

Chapter 8
The Return of Hell Cat

In the evenings, just before sunset, Preacher, Elaine, and Rot would visit their new house being constructed in a wooded area not far from the Ocala National Forest. It was not unusual for folk living on the road where Rot's house was located to see a flock of turkeys, some deer, or bear. Animals walking through the forest where they lived often went into the yards of housing residents.

Sometimes, Rot's pack drove north, down a road where their new house was being constructed, going to the far end of the road and, hooking around, went south to the lot of the new house. There were only ten houses in this development—five to the west and five to the east. Rot's house was the second one to the left off the main drive.

At the far end of the road, to the left, that is west, was a two-and-a-half-acre lot, large field with a forest at its back end and another road just beyond. At the end of that road, adjacent to this new area where houses would be constructed, was a dwelling where the residents fed raccoons and squirrels. One evening, Preacher spotted Hell Cat comfortably stretched out in the grass at the far end of the field. There are not many lions that still live in Florida. This discovery then was rather unusual.

Growing up in Philacanes, Preacher had often ridden with his Uncle Coon Honeywell, spotting deer just before dark. He recognized Hell Cat as a good-sized cougar. "Look," he said to Elaine and Rot, "there is a Florida lion lurking in that field. See it?"

Not only did Rot see Hell Cat, but Hell Cat saw Rot, and since the breeze was blowing from east to west, Hell Cat, being the predator that he was, picked up Rot's scent. It, by the way, is normal for animals being spotted from a car with the motor running to remain where they are. They see motor vehicles from their areas of sanctuary and know people operating such are going about their business and will leave them alone. It is when you turn your motor off or get out of your vehicle that they get alarmed, running away. So numerous evenings, Rot saw Hell Cat and, on a couple of occasions when the wind was blowing toward him, Rot picked up Hell Cat's scent. Hell Cat stayed in the area because he was being fed. And he had an additional reason for lingering about. Rot was still a puppy at the time, and visions of a juicy steak permeated Hell Cat's carnivorous skull.

Preacher, walking Rot on the same road, some days later, saw the tracks of Hell Cat in the lot across from the field in the wet dirt driveway of another new house just being constructed. "Yes," he said to Rot, "there is a Florida lion here. See the tracks? Here is one and here is another. He was walking going this way. Look, he's a big fellow."

Rot picked up the scent but at that time had no understanding of what Hell Cat was.

What Preacher did not know was that Hell Cat was often behind his house, in the foliage and heavy brush, out of sight, lurking, watching, waiting his opportunity to get the little dog. Later, Preacher's daughter and grandson would move into his home.

Early one morning, his daughter would arrive at the house and start to walk around from the drive on the sidewalk to the house front entrance and get startled half out of her wits by almost bumping into Hell Cat, walking toward her, coming from the opposite direction. Hell Cat, equally shocked, darted back the other way, while she returned to her car and called on her cell phone for Preacher to come get her. "What did you see?" asked Preacher.

"Well," said his daughter, "there wasn't much light, but there was a full moon, and I was almost to the yard lamp. But it was a large animal. It did not appear to be a dog. It was over knee-high. I think it was a big cat."

"Did it come after you?"

"No, but it scared me, and I think I scared it. I ran back the way I had come. It darted back the other way."

"Wow!" said Preacher. "I think I know what it was. Or should I say who it was!"

Chapter 9
Rot Witnesses Red's Death

Preacher was at work, and Rot was dozing comfortably stretched out in front of the sliding glass doors off the kitchen nook, facing the wooded area at the back end of the house. He was awakened by barking and shouting off to his right, the area in which he had been born. He could not see the altercation, so he ran to the laundry room window from which one could get a clear view of that area. Packed boxes of books prepared for the family's move to their new house were near the washer and dryer, so Rot, leaping on a stack of two of them, jumped to the top of the laundry room washer and looked out the window. Trees partially blocked his view of the burrow where he had been born, but he could clearly see the landscape leading up to it and the area above the tunnel that ran into the bank.

Rot recognized the short bulky man his master called Fitz and the tall lanky man he would later hear called Jake. He did not know what they were yelling, but he sensed they were bad words. Rot had heard tremendous howling. He had never heard anything like it before. For some reason, it stirred his blood. The hair on the back of his neck stood up. His tail arched up. His lips drew tight above his teeth. His wolfish incisors began to drip saliva. He was listening to the death song of a wolf—red dog, his mother. Somehow Rot understood.

Rot saw a long pole with a metal loop in the end of it. Fitz swung it evidently at red dog, and he must have missed because the next thing he knew, he could see red dog as she chased both Fitz and

Jake to their trucks. But she came back to her burrow. She had to do so, for she had five pups for which she would sacrifice her life.

Red, returning to her burrow, was followed by Fitz and Jake a few minutes later. There was rapid movement from all, yelling and cursing by Fitz, growling and nipping by Red. Finally, Rot saw Red with a firm hold on Fitz's right foot, a spray of red, and heard a scream of pain from Fitz. It was then that Jake hit Red behind her head with a shovel. Red collapsed. Fitz put the steel ring around her neck and, tightening it, choked her until she was dead.

Rot did not know Red was dead. He had never seen death before. While Red lay silently, Fitz and Jake jumped up and down on top of her burrow, whooping and shouting, gleefully laughing. Rot could not see exactly what they were doing, but he heard the cries of Red's puppies as one by one, they were stamped underneath the crumbling tunnel, until finally, there was no life in them.

All that is except for one that somehow managed to survive. Then Rot saw Fitz and Jake, holding them up one by one. Fitz, accompanying the stomping, choked the one that had lived with his bare hands. There were small yips until they ceased. Then Fitz dropped it and kicked it into the air.

Jake put the pups into a bag and started back to his truck with them. Fitz triumphantly, grinning from ear to ear, dragged Red off, whipping her dead body this way and that, over high weeds and little seedling trees. Now Fitz had a story of how he had fought off the attack of a vicious feral dog, choking it to death with his bare hands. His fellow workers would believe Fitz, no questions asked. It would furnish fodder for their prejudice against wild dogs and provide justification for acts of cruelty used in the performance of their duty, surreptitious activities believed necessary to deal with uncontrolled crude animals. What really happened must never be revealed to the public or other employees of the government. Red dog was vilified. Red was like the wolf children are told about by adults who constantly sing the chorus that wolves are evil and must be eliminated.

Rot saw all. Some dogs would have barked and barked. They do such with strangers, leery of their presence. But Rot did not bark. He had clearly witnessed an act of cruelty perpetuated against his mother, Red dog. From deep within Rot came a low seething growl. This event was fixated indelibly in his mind and would be a recurring nightmare in his dreams until he could come to a resolve in which his persona could find serenity.

Later that day, Preacher was told by the woman who had befriended Red dog that animal control had come and taken away Red and her five pups. Preacher went over to Red's burrow. He noted it had been collapsed, and the dogs were gone. Rot, unleashed, accompanying Preacher, using his redbone nose bred from the bloodhound to tell him what happened.

Rot smelled death. Sniffing here and there, he reconstructed the brutal scene of a few hours earlier. He clearly picked up the scent of Fitz and Jake. Again, a deep guttural growl seeped from his lips. It rolled on and on. Though young, a part of Rot's life was gone, like that which had happened with his mother, Red, years ago. But unlike with Red, Rot was secure. But Rot had an act of horror burned in his brain, seared in his mind. He would not forget. And often when he slept, he would cry out during the night. Such is the cry of an abused dog. These are the groans of creation, a creation that waits and looks for its glorious liberation to the coming of its Creator, and the bondage of our corruption is released with the glorious arrival of the sons of God.[1]

---

[1] The lion, a predator, hunts, eats, and then lies down and waits. All "Creation eagerly waits for the revelation of the sons of God" (Romans 8:19; paraphrased). "The creation was subjected to futility" (Romans 8:20). But the day is soon to come when "The creation itself will be delivered from the bondage of corruption into the glorious liberty of the children of God" (Romans 8:21; paraphrased). In that day, "The wolf shall dwell with the lamb. The leopard shall lie down with the young goat. The young lion and the calf will be together. The cow and the bear shall graze side by side. The lion shall eat straw. A child and a viper will play together enjoying the Lord's redeemed earth" (Isaiah 11:6–9).

Chapter 10
Winning a Friend

When Rot was eight months of age, he moved with his family from the rented quarters near where he was born to a new house, bordered by forest in its rear and with many oak trees on its lot. This was a real treat for those who had adopted him, for they were military retired and most of their career had lived in military housing.

Rot continued to thrive with daily attention from Preacher, rides in the red Jeep, various and sundry walks in local parks and a walking area in Glenwood, visits to a local dog park, and daily walks on the road on which his house was located. The road was owned by the residents whose houses filled the two-and-a-half-acre lots that were located on both sides. As such, it was semiprivate. Preacher had a cart built for his young grandson who now lived with him, and Rot would pull his grandson up their road, going north, and hook around south, returning him to their abode. The grandson, thrilled with this activity, would make the same circle again and again, almost daily. Rot loved the boy, and there are many photos of the two together. They had become the best of friends.

As time passed, Rot grew. Not only would Rot become a large dog, 125 pounds, but the rottweiler in him lent Rot to be a solid muscular canine. In addition, the continuing exercise of dog karate, and especially pulling his young friend in the dog-propelled cart developed rippling muscles in his legs, back, and shoulders. Often, when Preacher walked Rot downtown, a favorite activity of dog lovers with their dogs in this area, a common comment was, "That's not a dog. What you have there is a small horse."

Regular comments were, "That is a beautiful animal," "I like your dog," or "Where can I get a dog like that?" People riding by in cars or trucks would often slow down and make favorable comments.

One called Jake said to his friend Fitz, "That's the two-hundred-pound dog I was telling you about."

Fitz's comment was, "We've got to figure out how to get that dog. We can make a lot of money fighting him. Some of our friends would pay big-time to see what he can do."

At home, Dog Hawk and his brew continued to monitor Rot's walks with Preacher. As far as Dog Hawk knew, Rot did not know he existed. Dog Hawk himself became like a fixture in Rot's new domain. He could be seen on the roof of the house, often in the early morning, just over the west side of the great room, visible from Preacher's bedroom, or he could be seen on top of the basketball post that was north in the large cement driveway, or he could be seen on top of the large flagpole Preacher had at the north east end of his garage.

Dog Hawk became so comfortable lounging around that he began to light onto the field in front of Rot's house. East of the house, in front of it, about twenty yards away were two rows of large oaks, dispersed parallel with the road. Dog Hawk would fly in from his new home, now located in a tree southwest of Rot's house, where he and his brood could keep an eye on Rot. From various perches, he would locate to a tree in front of Rot's house and then end up in the good-sized mowed clearing. Preacher's lot was the only one among the houses on his road that had such. He would often bring the youth group from his church to play softball on the lot.

This particular day, Dog Hawk had spent some time in an oak tree near the mowed area of Rot's domain, looking for a squirrel, when he spread his great wings and coasted down to the ground in a comfortable stance. His impressive beaked head looked forward, then rotated this way and that, searching the landscape in total confidence that nothing could escape his flawless detection. Unknown to Dog Hawk, Rot had pushed down on the door latch to the back screened-in porch and was loose on the other side of the house. Rot, of course, through the windows in the twin doors at the house entrance, had seen Dog Hawk descend to the ground. He came around the south side of the house, out of sight, and slowly slinked behind a line of azaleas that ran toward the mowed field.

They were high enough to provide cover. Rot then slunk down behind some other landscape bushes and the oaks that happened to form a zag-type line behind Dog Hawk. Dog Hawk normally positioned himself with great precision and would never place himself in a way that allowed the trees behind him to form a line that could obscure another trying to sneak up on him. He had gotten so complacent that he often landed in the mowed area when Preacher was cutting the grass. When Preacher advanced toward the squatted hawk, he would just move a few feet hither or thither out of the way. Preacher, of course, liked the hawk and went out of his way not to disturb him. Dog Hawk, over time, lost all fear of Preacher. It never entered his mind to fear Rot. Rot, after all, though a mighty dog, was a creature of the ground, and Dog Hawk, one of the greatest of hawks, flew high above the greatest trees, far up into the heavens.

So it was that Rot crawling on his stomach, inched closer and closer a few feet at a time, until with a sudden burst of speed, he leaped past the last tree of cover, and with the great paws of his front feet, using them like hands, the hands that had opened the screen door, smacked Dog Hawk on his back side, pinning him fast to the ground. The air went out of Dog Hawks lungs. He could have rotated his head as hawks can do and tried to pick at Rot's eyes. But Dog Hawk was in such shock, his body so smacked flat on the grass, and the huge Rot so elevated above with huge white-bared teeth and guttural sounds coming deep from Rot's throat, that he, for a few minutes, became like his own victims—paralyzed. The two, for about three minutes, were frozen in time—Dog Hawk pinned flat on the ground, and Rot, 125 pounds of muscle, holding him in an inescapable grip of death. Rot could have torn off Dog Hawk's head.

Then an amazing smirk appeared on Rot's face. He released Dog Hawk, took a few steps backward, and lay down with his eyes upon the hawk. Rot's head remained high, his gaze intent. Rot was playing with Dog Hawk like he did in competition with Preacher. Dog Hawks blood began pouring back into the bruised parts of his body. He spread his wings and flapped them a few times. Everything appeared to be okay. Again, Dog Hawk flapped his wings, up he went and away.

Rot adopted the spot where he pinned Dog Hawk as the place in the front lawn that he would sit or mostly lay to watch who was coming or going on the road that ran in front of his territory. Preacher often let him alone to enjoy the fresh air of their country habitat and to enjoy his days on planet Earth. Then another amazing happening occurred after the Dog Hawk-Rot incident. The next day, Dog Hawk was in the largest oak on the property about fifteen yards from the previous day's episode. Rot came out and lay with his head held high, watching all like a hawk in the spot where he had pinned Dog Hawk. After about five minutes, Dog Hawk swooped down and squatted to the left of Rot. There, the two of them sat together, dog and hawk for about an hour.

At first it was just these two, enjoying the solitude of this quiet country setting. Eventually, Dog Hawk's son joined the two, and it was not long before all four hawks could be seen daily, sitting with Rot in the afternoon Florida sun. The mailman who visited the road's mail depository between the lanes in front of Preacher's domicile marveled at what he saw the first day and every day since. He told others of it, and sometimes, people would drive up and then back down the road to see the hawks and dog who were friends. But it was the great black dog and the great red hawk that impressed. They were seen together and often were so close, side by side, that they touched one another.

Chapter 11

Do Dogs Go to Heaven?

Preacher ate lunch on Tuesdays at a local barbecue restaurant with a couple of preachers from another area church. This Tuesday, his friend, Kevin, who had two labs as pets, was joking him about the talk of his dog, Rot, and the hawks that sat by Rot in his commodious front yard. Another pastor, Joel, said the scenario reminded him of Isaiah chapter 11, about a time promised when in the millennium, the wolf would lie with the lamb, the leopard with the goat, the lion would eat straw like an ox, the nursing child play by the cobra's hole, and a weaned child could put its hand in a viper's hole. None would be hurt or destroyed. The talk then swung around to the question, do animals go to heaven?

Kevin said, "God has a special concern for animals. Note in Jonah when the prophet was comforted because God caused a plant with a large leaf to shade him as he waited in the hot sun of Nineveh for God to destroy the Assyrians. Then God caused a worm to destroy the plant. Jonah was angry and wanted to die. God asked Jonah if it was right for him to be angry about the plant, even to the point of death. God led Jonah to see his foolishness by asking, 'Should I not be concerned about Nineveh, a city of one hundred and twenty thousand people who cannot discern between their right hand and their left—and much livestock?' I emphasize the livestock. God did not want the animals of the Assyrians to suffer. I think that indicates God wants animals saved." Note in Psalm 36:6, the Scripture records, "O Lord, You preserve man and beast."

There were always people sitting at nearby booths who listened in on the conversation as they ate and especially subjects of this sort. It was not unusual for the preachers, when they got to the cash register following the consumption of their tasty vitals, to find that some listener had paid for their meal. The cashier often had a message of appreciation that customers wanted passed on to the preachers. Many commented favorably about the prayer the preachers prayed in public in thanksgiving for their food and for the welfare of their community and country.

Joel added, "When the Israelites were in Egypt, and God brought plagues against Pharaoh, He made an exception among the Hebrews, and He protected their animals as well. In Exodus 11:7, during the last plague, animals were singled out for deliverance as well as the people."

"Well," said Preacher, "as you indicate, all through the Bible, we see God's special affection for the animals of His creation, but the best scripture for their salvation is the account of Noah and the Flood."

Someone from the booth across the aisle from the one in which the pastors was eating blurted out, "How so?" Then she apologized, saying, "I am sorry. My friend and I are captivated by your discussion. We are both dog lovers, and we are Christians. What is there about the story of Noah that would teach us anything about salvation for animals?"

"The Bible," said Preacher, "is full of types. A type is a historical fact that illustrates a spiritual truth. The ark is a type of salvation. Only those in the ark were saved. The people in the ark saved through a universal flood were Noah and his wife and his three sons and their wives—eight people. God determined who was to be saved. When Noah and his family entered the ark, God shut them in—that is, God closed the door."

"Okay, I'm Victoria, by the way, and this is Emily, my sister. So what about the animals? Your dog and his friends, the hawks?"

"Yes," said the Preacher. "I'm coming to that. As you know, the ark was full of animals. Some of these animals were to provide food for Noah and other animals during the flood. But there were two of every kind of animal that God saved from the flood. These were released after the flood to repopulate the earth. Now the point on the animals, plugging into the 'type analysis,' is that God selected the animals to be saved and brought them to Noah. Here again, note God selected the animals that were indeed saved. Those saved came to Noah and experienced the preservation of their lives in the ark."

Kevin inserted, "It makes sense to me. We could say the ark was a type of Christ. All pronounced by Jesus as righteous or imputed with righteousness. As was Noah, the Scripture noting he became heir of righteousness, which is according to faith are in the Lord, our ark of deliverance."

"And," said Preacher, "if the Lord who is our Creator, and the earth is His as it is taught in Psalm 24:1 and other places in the Scripture, chooses to deliver certain animals to other realms beyond earth as He delivered animals through the Great Flood, such is His prerogative."

"That could be another instance," said Joel, "where the Lord, in His Goodness as He promises in Psalm 37:4, to give those who delight in Him the desires of our hearts, reunites those who loved their pets with them somehow or other in celestial realms."

"Piggybacking on what has already been said," Preacher added, "God made a covenant with Noah when he and his family came out of the ark. The covenant was for all Noah's descendants and every living creature that was with him on the ark, the birds, the cattle, and every beast of the earth that Noah had on the ark. God was definitely indicating that animals were special to Him, and this He has demonstrated to us through Noah and the ark, the following covenant, and the rest of Scripture as the Provider and Sustainer of all life on our planet."

"Amen," said Kevin.

"Amen," said Joel.

"Amen," said Victoria.

"Amen," said Emily.

"Amen," said the Preacher.

"Amen," said another to the right of the booth in which the pastors were sitting.

To the right of their booth and to all booths in that line was a low wall with slide-in wood separators between each booth so two tables could be joined as one and eight customers could be accommodated, four in each booth. A tall man on the opposite side of their booth had said, "Amen."

"What's your name?" asked Kevin.

The fellow whose head could be seen over the separation between the booths said, "Jake."

The sneering man opposite Jake said, "Garbage."

Chapter 12

A Deadly Fellow

Preacher, his wife, daughter, and grandson were ready to go to church Sunday morning. Opening the left of the large double doors in front of his house, Preacher attempted to step outside. Rot, however, from his right side, muscled his way in front of him and would not let him pass. Being the 125pound muscular animal that he was, it meant pretty well that Preacher was not going out the front door. If Rot was saying, "Do not move," you did not move.

Preacher did not know what to say. Rot had never done anything like this before, and the behavior seemed foreign to him. He even moved forward, pushing Preacher a few steps further back into the house. Then he commenced to growl and to raise his lips, displaying awesome teeth. Some rottweilers are intimidating, and to say such of this dog was no exaggeration.

It was observed that Rot's tail was not wagging. Instead, it was erect, pointing upward. Trusting this great dog and knowing him well, Preacher looked through the doorway and beyond. There, on the sidewalk where he would have stepped, was a black, red, and yellow striped snake, the largest of this kind that Preacher had even seen. If Preacher had continued his forward momentum before Rot intervened, he would have stepped right on the snake.

Preacher's daughter, Corlissa, behind him, blocked from going out the door by Rot and her dad, asked, "What is happening? Why aren't we going out the front door?"

Preacher, raising his right arm, pointing his index finger at the snake, said, "Look."

Soon, his wife Elaine, and his grandson, David, were also looking.

Preacher said, "Look at that snake's head. It's black."

Some days earlier he and Corlissa had been working in the flower garden in the right front area of the house facing the road, and there right before them lay a ringcolored snake. Corlissa had asked, "Is this a coral snake?"

"No," Preacher replied, "it's a scarlet snake. Notice it has a scarlet-colored head? A coral snake has a black head." He continued, "Leave this snake alone. It isn't hurting anybody."

He could remember as a young boy a neighbor who he often visited who had a farm with many animals and numerous buildings of chickens. They were clearing away some brush in high ferns. The kindly elderly man's right foot stepped on a large black snake. The snake's head loomed toward the man's right leg, but the snake did not bite. The neighbor said, "Dick, never kill a snake. A snake is the farmer's friend. Snakes eat rats, and rats kill chickens." The neighbor took his foot off the snake, and it slithered away. And of course, as taught, Preacher did not kill snakes.

"Well," said Corlissa, "is that a coral snake?"

Preacher replied, "Yes, it is! The saying goes, Red touches black, safe for Jack. Red touches yellow, kills a fellow, or as some people put it, dangerous fellow." Long before Preacher had ever seen a coral snake while in high school in Pennsylvania, his football coach, a reserve lieutenant JD in the navy, a scuba diver, talking to a few players, which included Preacher, spoke of a summer assignment in Florida. He had been told if a coral snake bit him, to sit down and smoke a cigarette because it was all over. By the time he finished his smoke, he would be dead.

There are four poisonous snakes in Florida. Three, the rattlesnake (there are numerous kinds), cottonmouth (water moccasin), and copperhead are front-fanged snakes. The fourth, the coral snake, is a rear-fanged snake (like the cobra). What that means is the coral snake, which is characteristically a docile snake, when biting you, latches unto you and injects into you all its venom. The consequence is that usually such a bite kills a human. Preacher had one practice regarding a coral snake—do not take any chance with it.

Most people think coral snakes are small thin snakes. Corlissa thought so. Later, Preacher and his daughter looked up the coral snake on the Internet, and Preacher was able to show what he already knew. Coral snakes grow to be three feet long, and these are not small thin snakes.

As they stared at the snake, Preacher commented to Corlissa, "Look at the rings on this snake. See the red rings touch the yellow—dangerous fellow. It's remarkable to me that Rot called our attention to this snake and that he knew its danger. I have seen black snakes crawl in our field near the road, right by him, and he never seemed aware of them. It is obvious the whole time he ignored them, he knew they were there. The animal world is so amazing—mysterious. How did this dog know what a coral snake is?"

So the snake, being just outside from the front door, Elaine asked, "Now what do we do?"

Rot, who knew many words—like come, walk, mail, here, eat, nap, no, drink, attack, sit, lay, stay, up, quiet, look, beef stick, and many more, some less appropriate to reference, seem to know, as on many occasions, exactly what Elaine had said. Rot rotated, now facing the snake only a few feet away. Rot, his total persona focused on the snake, acting as the family's protector, a guard dog extraordinaire, eyeball-to-eyeball, began to growl and bark aggressively. "Move," he barked. "And move right now!"

The coral snake, apparently threatened, slowly began to slide with a zigzag movement into the red bark area just off to the left of the sidewalk. There it lay as if it knew how deadly it was. It was going no further. And nobody was going to walk by it—either.

It was unusual for Rot to bark as he was. Rot was not prone to fits of barking when someone came to the front door and rang the doorbell. His demeanor was one of calm. Maybe it was the wolf in him. Wolves can and do bark but seldom. He was not threatened by other dogs. He mostly ignored them. Rot's size and spirit was such that he was a dog of great confidence, and he was not inclined to assert himself. But bark he did, and again, one who lived in his household would wonder what he was doing.

Only a few minutes passed, and low in the sky, from the east, came into view a low flying great redwing hawk. The eye of a hawk is such that he can pinpoint the smallest object from high in the sky. Dog Hawk—we now use that term affectionately—flew swiftly, increasing in size and visibility as he came nearer, swooped down in a pinpoint dive, snatched up Deadly Fellow in his great talons, and was last seen winging swiftly back eastward with the black, red, and yellow dangerous fellow dangling helplessly below. Snakes dangling in the air—not grounded, are completely disadvantaged, at the mercy of their transporter. In a matter of seconds, the great hawk was gone, and the snake incident was like a mirage. However, it was not a mirage—it really happened.

Chapter 13
The Visitation

The red Jeep, C5 with the eight-cylinder engine, was driven north on I-95 from Daytona through Jacksonville and on into Georgia. Rot rode to the right of Preacher on the right front seat, strapped in by his own seat belt styled by Preacher. It was arranged to give him some movement, and he could look out the window to the right, ahead, to the left, or if he whined, be unleashed and ride on the back seat where he could look in multiple directions or sleep. He, however, for the most part, preferred to look at the scenery as they rode and seemed to be in deep anticipation. Somehow, God speaks to animals, whether it is time for the bear to hibernate, the salmon to swim upstream to lay eggs for offspring, or a lion to slay a disobedient prophet and to stay by his body, guarding it, not bothering the prophet's donkey or anyone else, until the servant of God is taken away, and the lion is released from duty. Mankind who thinks he is so sophisticated has such little knowledge in these matters.

Preacher did not need to, but he stopped at a Sonny's on the exit to Saint Augustine because he had become friends with the owner. They had met in a previous trip, and Preacher had given his new-found friend a card with his name, address, and phone number along with the name of a book he had written. Rot was introduced to the owner. They struck up an immediate camaraderie.

Continuing, they stopped off I-95 at Pope Air Force Base, where they spent the night in a TLQ (temporary living quarters) unit. Preacher and Rot had supper with some old friends from the time his family lived on base, and he served as a chaplain. They reminisced about Preacher's earlier ministry when he had a unique Volkswagen painted like an airplane with God Squad in golden letters written on the side. Here, Rot was a big hit with these newfound friends—performing numerous commands from Preacher to perfection.

After numerous pit stops at roadside rests, they arrived in Philacanes, where Preacher and Rot were met by various family members at his former domicile some three hundred yards down the mountainside, east of the house and barn of Red, Rot's mother. The family was amazed by a dog karate demonstration in which Rot pinned Preacher, as he had done in North Carolina at Pope AFB. Though it was late March in Pennsylvania, March often comes in like a lion and goes out like a lamb. The day was sunny and beautiful, so the family had a cookout while they discussed the business for which Preacher had made a journey northward.

Meanwhile, Rot ventured north into the forested area bordering the family land. This was the roaming area of Red during the first year of her life. Rot, himself now two years old, drank from the creek, discovered the area where deer traversed, the mountain laurel when Red often laid, and going further up the mountain, came to an old barn with a wagon wheel leaning against it on its southside. For some reason, he had an overpowering urge to push the wheel further out because of his size and lie under it. Facing west where he could observe the black top road past the barn, he dropped off into a pleasant sleep—dreaming of Preacher and their present wondrous trip.

Rot, sensing a presence, remaining perfectly still, opened his eyes, focusing on a huge silver wolf larger than him. The wolf made no move. He just continued to stare. Rot slowly rose. The wolf stepped back, and Rot stepped forward. Neither made a sound. Then they checked each other out. The silver stepped back a few spaces with an intense concentration on Rot. As he turned west, he twisted his head to the right back toward Rot and proceeded to render a short series of yips. Rot understood he was to follow.

Across the road ahead, they went up the bank to the right, through some great fields, to a forest line of pines, and further on to the left, up an old road over a rise, down into a dip, and up the incline to where the land leveled out some distance before the state preserve beyond. After the dip and over the incline lay a great pack of wolves. They all rose as the Great Silver and Rot approached.

It was obvious the silver was the leader of this pack. All stood at attention. Then a great white and a smaller red wolf, bearing unmistakable similarity to Rot's mother, Red, slowly approached from the far west perimeter. The Queen steadily gazed at Rot as she slowly approached. She sniffed his nose and other vital areas, as had the Great Silver. Then she stood before him and licked his face. There was no doubt. He was one of them. He was the son of Red. The great white did the same.

Now all the wolves were whimpering, moaning, and groaning. Incredibly, some knew of El, and most knew Red. Rot was receiving bumps, rubs, and licks from all members of the pack. He, too, seemed to know. What a great day it was for the pack! What a great day it was for Rot. As it reads in Isaiah 63:14, "The Holy Spirit, Spirit of God, gives animals rest, or God comforts his beasts, the beasts of the forest."

Then, suddenly, it was over. The Great White and Queen headed northwest hastily, treading into the great reserve followed by the rest of their pack. The Great Silver again beckoned Rot, and they went north for some distance. It is possible that Rot could have gone with the pack, but he never gave it a thought. The pack seemed to have something else in mind. Unknown to Rot, the pack remained some distance to his west, monitoring his movement along a creek. The Great Silver had something he wished to show Rot. This done and understood, in short order, the Silver and Rot returned to the barn with the leaning wagon wheel.

The Silver licked Rot in the face, and then he raised his face to the heavens. Out came a great howl, the howl of the wolf, the howl of the great northern pack, the howl of Red's pack, a howl for this developing enigma, a howl for Rot and his discovery of his pack, a howl for the pack and their introduction to Rot, and a howl to the Creator, known to this pack and every critter. From high on the mountain to the west came a response; the sonorous yowl of many denizens of the wild. Rot had heard howling from his mother when she had given her death cry. He had never understood. Now he raised his face to the heavens, and he gave his first howl. It was deep, loud, and clear—sonorous. The wolves from the mountain answered. Rot licked the Silver in the face. That was it.

Preacher and his family heard it all. Preacher said, "Where is Rot?"

The answer from all, one by one, was, "I do not know."

And then Rot was there. "Here he is," someone said.

So the big Rot's first great adventure, a providential trip, was soon complete. And he, by and by, found himself back home, enjoying the boundaries of his private domain and the persons of his household.

Chapter 14
Hell Cat's New Perspective

Hell Cat had been lurking behind Rot's domicile off and on since his family moved into their new home. The forest and Florida undergrowth, some one hundred and fifty feet behind the house, was like a jungle thick with vines that wrapped around the trees and assortments of aquatic plants. Earlier, he had hoped to catch the Rot off guard when family members were dosing or not close by. But Rot had grown into a large dog, and beside that, Hell Cat could not help but notice that the dog was ripped with muscle and had a dominant personality. In truth, his persona was such that to some, Rot was quite scary.

In the course of his pursuit, Hell Cat had eaten a few strays that people had dropped along the road. One dog he stole from a five-foot chain-linked fenced in the area. The fence was not an obstacle to Hell Cat. The family lived on the street behind Rot's land and on the other side of the trees and thick vegetation. They had gone somewhere and left their young shepherd in the backyard. Hell Cat easily sailed over the fence and quickly made his kill. The young shepherd, the kind of prey this cat sought, an animal lacking any kind of maturity and ability to give a good fight, was carried back over the fence. The family grieved and puzzled about their dog's disappearance. They had no clue as to what had happened.

Now Rot was back from his first trip and great adventure in which he had contacted the most fearsome of his mother's family. He had not had opportunity to renew his friendship with Dog Hawk and his family. Hell Cat, this day, still hanging around, was south of Rot's house, off to the right, toward the roadway used by the houses of this new housing development. In the strip of woods that connected the brush of the forest behind Rot's dwelling and ran to the roadway, Hell Cat laid close to the ground. He had not seen Rot for some days. The skilled stalking predator was not visible. He had been eyeing another dog, a Jack Russel that lived in Rot's abode, the pet of Preacher's daughter. Hell Cat did not know the dog was horrendously feisty, but it would not have mattered because the dog was small, and Hell Cat knew it would be no match for him. The cat had noticed Feisty was let out at a certain time every afternoon in the front yard and left alone while it sniffed around wandering here and there on the grounds, enjoying its territory.

The Preacher's daughter had not been living with her parents, and when she came to do so, Feisty came with her.

Rot met Feisty at the door. It, of course, was Rot's territory. Feisty's greeting to Rot was to give him three quick nips in the face. Rot, of course, could have bitten Feisty's head off with one bite, but he did not respond. In fact, Rot normally would not bite a female dog or engage one in any kind of hostility against it. It was not long before the two were the best of friends. Rot often deferred to Feisty. Frequently, you could see them lying up against each other, and they took turns licking the others' face.

Hiding in a strip of wood that runs from point A, which is a woodland area where animals hide, and connects to another strip, on the other side of a road, running back to another area of concealment; point B is something all kinds of animals do in stealth. Deer do it quite skillfully. Animals are exceedingly intelligent. Preacher remembers, when ministering in a rural area in Virginia, one buck season, visiting a store owner in an area heavily hunted, where the proprietor was greatly amused, across the road from the store was a bank with some clover on it. To the back of it was a brush wood line. Hunters would stop at the store to buy food, drinks, ammunition for their guns, and various other items.

When the hunters purchasing items would depart, a large buck with many points would come out of the brush and eat clover. When another car or truck would approach, the buck would hurriedly slink into the woods where it was hidden from sight. The store owner never did tell the hunters about the deer. It was his secret and the deer's. Obviously, the deer knew the man was watching and did not see him as a threat, for he had adjusted to the man's presence.

Rot was back. Feisty was let out, and this day, Hell Cat, who knew his routine, was waiting for her to come by that part of the grounds where he lay in wait. He was hungry, and this was the day he had chosen to pounce upon the small animal. However, there was one small problem for Hell Cat. Or maybe it was a big problem. Because all the days Hell Cat lay nearby, Rot knew he was there. The redbone is descended from the bloodhound. Rot looked like a rot and was a rot, but he had the nose of a bloodhound and the cunning of a great white wolf. He could remember when he was a pup, and his mother was hiding in a field of high grass nearby, he knew she was there. Rot knew Hell Cat liked to lay in that stretch of woods and suspected he might be there.

He pressed down on the handle of the left front door of his house and let himself out. Having gone ten or so feet, he knew Hell Cat was there. He picked up his scent. The wind was coming from the direction of Hell Cat, and the fact that he could not be seen did him no good. And Hell Cat could not smell Rot. Neither could he see him because Rot approached behind the great oaks in front of the house. He, too, knew stealth, the same way he had stalked Dog Hawk. The great-grandson of the great white wolf hunched down and swiftly scooted forward.

Feisty had gone toward the wood line and had swung around. She was near the road and facing away from Hell Cat. Hell Cat had come from the woody area and was inching forward. His mind was wholly on the small dog in front of him. Then he raised his head in disbelief. Down the road came a small partially clad barefooted girl, blonde hair, about three years old. Hell Cat could not believe his good fortune. His eyes were now riveted on this new object of opportunity. In all the days of his life, he had never had such good fortune.

Why do things happen like they do? Normally, when going to town, you get some red lights and some green. Today, you are behind schedule, and you get every red light. You always have your wallet. You are military and know you must always have your ID. For twenty years, you never failed to have your identification. But today, in your hurry, you changed pants and forgot to switch your wallet to the pants you are wearing. And today is the day the police stop you for going five miles over the speed limit. You go to the post office and do not put on your security alarm because you will only be gone half an hour. You also forget to put your garage door down. Coming home, you find all your Christmas presents gone. Jake the Rake has not cased your home in the last six months, but this happened to be the day he came by, and he scored big-time.

The little girl from the family across the street has never got out of her house unnoticed, but today with Hell Cat in the strip of woods near your house, she is walking down your road right in front of him. Disaster lurks in your nearby woods.

Preacher, still on vacation, just happened to walk into the great room and noticed the left front door was open. Assuming Rot had opened it, he stepped outside to see what was happening. Taking a few steps with a linebacker's vision, he espied the little girl on the road, Feisty in the field nearby, Hell Cat creeping toward the girl, and Rot. Suddenly, Rot launched forward like a ball fired from a cannon. Preacher could not even see his legs beneath him. He looked like a cannonball fired from a great gun.

Hell Cat, totally absorbed with the little girl as the grandest prize ever, and somewhat hesitant because he knew it was wrong to attack a human, did not see the rocket propelling toward him. The resounding thud was awesome. Rot blindsided the big cat, hitting him on his left side, smacking him some ten yards. At the same time, Rot was biting him in multiple areas, above the left shoulder, behind his head, and in his neck. Some ribs were broken, and he could not get up. He was stunned. It was unusual for such a large lion to be so discombobulated, but Rot was a large dog, exceptionally muscular, only slightly removed from a wolf heritage.

Rot could have killed Hell Cat, but he didn't. When Hell Cat did not get up, Rot followed the little girl who had decided to return to her house. Rot stopped at the roadside, while the little girl entered the garage from which she had excited. She went back into the laundry room through the doorway through which she had previously come when she pushed the unsecure door open. Rot then checked out Feisty who, for once, had nothing to contribute but had beat a retreat to the slow advancing Preacher. Hell Cat slowly got up and reentered the strip of woods, the hiding place from which he had come.

For the next two weeks, he continued where he was. Preacher graciously brought him water and canned dog food. Every day, Rot came by to check on him. This time, Rot did acknowledge his presence. Hell Cat went through a behavioral modification, Rot being the instrument conditioning him concerning an unacceptable payoff. This lion was carnivorous, but he learned, as he already knew, and now was reinforced on him, never stalk a human. He also understood from an earlier experience with two other dogs, and now this one, do not eat dogs. They are friends with humans, and it can be painful to mess with them. And contrary to what one may have expected, Hell Cat, when healed, did not disappear, never to be seen again. Hell Cat did go back to the national forest, but from time to time, reappeared, hiding from others, but not from Preacher or the big Rot.[2, 3, 4]

---

[2] The Florida panther is a subspecies of cougar. Males can weigh up to 161 pounds.

[3] I remember reading years ago in the *Reader's Digest* about a high school runner killed and partially eaten by a cougar while running behind his high school in Colorado. The cougar was found and killed.

[4] Reporting on cougars in Washington, it is noted they are also called mountain lions. It is observed they rarely attack humans. About twenty-five people have been killed since officials began tracking attacks a hundred years ago. I read of numerous attacks on humans, especially children.

Chapter 15

The Day of Rot Begins

Rot's experience with Hell Cat meant he was now ready to settle an old score. It had been over two weeks since that incident, and Hell Cat had gone back to the wild. Rot had renewed his friendship with Dog Hawk and his brood. This day, they sat in front of the two-tier wood line, oak trees in front of Rot's house. There were four hawks, a young falcon, and Dog Hawk's mate on Rot's left, and on his right, Dog Hawk, and a tierce, his son, Swift Hawk. They were all enjoying a Florida beautiful sunny day, and for all, it was a time of repose.

A red pickup truck drove up the road in front of Rot's residence, circled around at the end of the lane where the last houses were on the right and left, and proceeded back down the road. It stopped in front of Rot's domain. The window on the passenger side was rolled down, and Fitz stuck a rifle barrel out, leaned his right elbow on the window frame, looked through the scope, and shot his twenty-two, hitting the tierce hawk, Swift Hawk, next to Dog Hawk. The young hawk fell over. Jake the Rake hit the accelerator, and the pickup moved to the end of the road, stopping at the stop sign. Rot, sniffing the fallen hawk, turned and jetted down the lane in pursuit of the truck. The truck turned right and proceeded down Glenwood Road. Rot followed.

Rot knew about red lights. He walked every Sunday through DeLand, Preacher instructing him to stay on the sidewalks and not to cross the road until the light at the intersection was green. The red truck crossed 15A because the light was green, and Rot also made it through the green light. Rot continued to follow, while the truck driver made sure he did not go so fast as to lose him.

After a short distance, the truck turned unto a dirt road into a compound surrounded by a six-foot chain-linked fence. Rot followed the truck into the enclosure, much to the delight of the two men in the truck. Fitz produced a remote, pushed a button on it, and the gate electronically closed. By now, he was gloating so badly that his face was a crimson red, and slobber was running from his lips.

Already, Dog Hawk with some of his extended family was circling above the few buildings with the surrounding fence. *Keeia, keeia, keeia*, they cried. Their commotion was oblivious to Fitz. Meanwhile, Rot was digging a hole in the dirt drive, and there was a rising pile of dirt in front of the gate. "Look at that stupid dog!" cried Fitz. "He is too dumb to know his fix."

Jake the Rake was ordered to bring two fighting dogs up to work the big Rot over. "Do not kill him," Fitz ordered. "We will rough him up and teach him to fight."

The dogs were commanded to attack. Rot, continuing to dig his hole and to pile up dirt, sidestepped the first attacking dog. It fell into the hole. The second dog was met by a brutal frontal attack that turned it around, fleeing for the building from which it had come. The other dog, crawling out of the hole, was thrown back in and chose to stay there.

Fitz, now in a fit of rage, ordered Jake the Rake to bring Killer. Meanwhile, Fitz had a sturdy stick about six feet long. He ran at Rot and tried to hit him with the stick. Fitz brought the stick down with tremendous blow right over Rot, but Rot stepped to the right, easily avoiding it. Fitz tried three more times, each time becoming more frustrated because he could not even touch this dog. Finally losing all sense of sanity, he ran at Rot, kicking with his right leg, trying to smash Rot in the face. Fitz's leg thrust violently thrown was so vicious that he lost control of his body. Fitz's right leg high in the air, losing balance, his left leg went out from beneath him, and he fell down on his back in front of Rot. In a panic, he rolled to the left and ended up in the hole Rot had dug. The pit, still in the hole, bit him.

Rot, meanwhile, was where he had been all along—close to the pile of dirt he had deposited in front of the gate. Out of the dog barracks came Killer. He did not have to be ordered to attack. He charged at Rot full speed, which, for him, was not all that fast. Rot did not move. With incredible speed, like a professional boxer who easily penetrates his opponent's defense and skillfully lands a power punch right on his jaw, his huge powerful jaws latched on to Killer's jaws, above and beneath, and using Killer's own momentum, he threw Killer up in the air, Rot twisting his huge powerful neck to the left, snapped Killer's neck. In so doing, Killer was thrown to the left. Rot released him. Killer fell dead, at last getting a taste of what he had dispensed to many other dogs.

Fitz, by now, was in a state of hysteria. At this point, he was no longer determined to use Rot in fights to make money. He simply wanted this dog, like his grandmother, her pups, and his mother, Red, dead. He ordered Jake the Rake to get the other dogs. Rot ran toward Fitz, purposively, slowly. Out of the hole, Fitz retreated hastily to further in the compound. Rot lingered until he saw the other dogs and Jake the Rake. Rot remembered the scent from the scene of his mother's demise. He knew who these men were and what he was doing. Seeing the Rake and the approaching dogs, although he had followed Fitz twenty or so yards into the compound, he turned and ran toward the gate. "Stupid dog!" screamed Fitz.

Rot, Fitz's rod in his teeth, at a good speed, leaped from off the pile of dirt, giving him an advantage in the height of his leap, and easily sailed over the gate. Outside the gate, he paused, looking at the dogs, Fitz, and Rake. He dropped Fitz's rod and gave a short series of ridiculing barks, and to his own surprise, a challenging howl, and down the road he trotted, toward his own abode.

Out of the gate came the red pickup truck loaded with three other fighting dogs in the bed, Fitz and Jake the Rake in the cab with their twenty-two. This time, they were following Rot, who, though these men did not know it, was now in charge.

Along the roadway, to the left, someone had hired the construction of a new house. To the right of the structure were many cement blocks like those that had been used in the building of Rot's house.

Rot left the road and ran to the left, jumping upon the pile of blocks. There he sat, visible to those in the red truck. Fitz could have shot Rot, but he wanted to watch his dogs tear Rot apart.

The red pickup pulled off the road. It appeared no one was present. The three fighting dogs were released. Rot moved a little to the right, down the elongated pile. Up came the dogs, jumping onto the blocks. Soon, the first, second, and third had their legs caught in the holes in the blocks. In their haste and effort to attack Rot, they made their predicament worse. One dog broke a leg. One got out of his present dilemma to chase Rot. Rot moved over more blocks, athletically experienced from earlier exercises, carefully not allowing his legs to slip into holes. The dog pursuing, again, got a leg in a hole and wrenching it to get to Rot, pulled a muscle. The third dog, giving up not trying to extricate itself, was shot by Fitz who had little tolerance for inefficiency in his animals. The two dogs, needing assistance and no longer of any use in the effort to subdue Rot, were left to their own means for survival.

Fitz would have shot at Rot, but Rot, seeing a ladder against the single-story house, had jumped off the block pile before Fitz approached and went up the ladder, rung by rung, and stood glaring at Fitz and Jake the Rake from the house roof. Fitz said to Jake, "Now we have him. Climb that ladder and knock that dog off the roof."

Jake exclaimed, "Me?"

Fitz impatiently yelled, "Yea, you! Do it NOW!"

Rot waited, watching Jake until he was almost at the top of the ladder, then he came forward and pushed Jake back on the ladder with his forehead and the great strength of his thick neck and muscle-toned body. Jake fell backward, screaming as he went landing, ladder and all on Fitz. After some minutes, Rot, sitting and watching the two buffoons below as they scrambled and rolled about, noting that Fitz had found his rifle, moved over the roof to the other side. There he jumped off the roof and ran into the forest behind the house. While Fitz and Jake the Rake, having walked to the backside of the house, stood in puzzlement, trying to contemplate where Rot could be. He barked three brief barks, "Hey, guys, I'm over here."

RICHARD BESTEDER

Fitz and Jake the Rake went back up the road to their dog fighting facilities. There they got supplies and money and their last two dogs and their only two bloodhounds purchased from a neighbor on Rot's street who had moved away. They returned to the new house construction and found Rot waiting for them in a field in front of the forest just beyond the house. As they pulled up in their red truck, Rot remained in sight but maintained a good distance from them so as not to be shot by Fitz. Incensed even more, Fitz released his bloodhounds in pursuit of Rot. He was bound and determined to destroy that dog. Fitz knew he was the son of Red. He had killed Eleanor and her pups, and that blasted Red dog. And now it would be the greatest endeavor of his life—to eliminate Rot.

Chapter 16

Headed North

Bloodhounds are amazing trackers. Slave owners used them in the days of slavery to track runaway slaves. When bloodhounds were in pursuit, it was difficult to escape. Earlier, Jake the Rake had stolen some items from Rot's household, one of them being a mat on which Rot used to sleep. It was used to provide scent the hounds needed to catch their prey. The large strong dogs each had leather harnesses with long leather leashes held by Jake the Rake so they didn't get too far ahead, thus getting lost in the brush.

Going was hard—through a tangle of young trees interspersed with myriads of thin vines, many underleaves and various and sundry types of plants, some of it poison ivy. As the party went along, there were fallen trees and branches, large and small, having dropped off large oaks scattered everywhere. Jake the Rake, an uncoordinated comedy of gyrations, whirling and spinning this way and that as he was jerked forward by the enthusiastic hounds, did much better than Fitz, for the Rake was tall and able to step over many small bushes and tangles. Fitz, in shorts, did not realize it, but he already had poison ivy over much of his legs. He had fallen twice, having tripped over ground vines that seemed to jerk his feet viciously out from under him. Short and overweight and not used to such physical exertion, he was huffing and puffing as he struggled onward. Then, too, there were the snakes. Fitz stepped on a black racer. The snake did not bite, but Fitz's fear was worse than the bite. He could be heard uttering over and over, "I hate snakes."

Meanwhile, Dog Hawk with six other hawks flew overhead. *Keeia, keeia, keeia,* they cried. Dog Hawk would dive, threatening toward Fitz and Jake. His friends did the same. The incensed hawk took Fitz's hat right off his head. Fitz drew his pistol, shooting at the hawks but not hitting any.

They had only gone a difficult couple of miles when Fitz concluded this rot is not returning home. "According to my compass, he is bypassing his house. What is he doing? Is he lost? He is one stupid dog! I cannot go on like this! I am going back to the truck and get on roads that will follow a course parallel to you. We will communicate by cell phone. When he comes out of the woods, we will get him. I am going to make him pay for this!"

Fitz's decision was not democratic. When had he ever sought Jake's input? Jake was like, "But, but, but."

With that, Fitz was gone. The Rake was yanked in the opposite direction. He could swear, off in the distance, every so often, he saw a large black dog ahead, waiting for them. The dog would pause and then move once again out of sight.

It was some time before Jake's cell phone rang. He had taken numerous breathers. The dogs were not well. "Is that you, Fitz?" the Rake asked.

"Who did you think it was?" said Fitz. "The preacher? You're almost as stupid as that dumb dog. Jake," said Fitz, "you like to go to Dustin's and listen to those pastors talk."

"Yea," replied Rake, "I like to hear what they say about God. Until I started listening to them, I didn't know anything about God."

"I don't care anything about God!" yelled Fitz.

"Yea, I know," Rake muttered.

"What I want to know is, did that preacher say anything about the trip up north with his dog? Did he mention any stops? Like that dog may have it in his head to go back to Philacanes!"

"Yea, yea," said Rake. "Sitting in the booth off to their left, I heard all about it."

"Well, out with it, out with it. Quit stalling and tell me what was said!"

"Yea, the preacher likes barbecue. Yea, he had a friend who owns a Sonny's just off the Saint Augustine exit. After Preacher returned from his trip, I heard him say he stopped at Sonny's and his dog had become a friend with the owner."

"Ah," said Fitz. "I'm headed for Sonny's! I know an animal control person there. I will call him, and we will intercept that stupid dog. He is so dumb!"

"But, but," said the Rake, "what about me?"

"Where are you?" demanded Fitz.

"I'm somewhere past DeLand," said the Rake. "In the forest north of 92, toward Daytona. And I have these two dogs. Yea, yea, they're hungry and exhausted, and so am I," said the Rake.

"Got to go," said Fitz.

That was it. The Rake was alone with the two bloodhounds. They had crossed numerous small streams of water. The Rake's pants were strewn with mud and ripped in two places. Perspiration beaded his head. His shirt was wet with sweat. He knew he stank. Mosquitoes were everywhere. The Rake would take off his camouflaged baseball hat and repeatedly swipe at them. At least when it remained on his head, it gave him partial protection.

The hawks were gone. Dog Hawk thought, *You are going to deal with my big friend, Rot. You do not know what you are doing. He will avenge me for Swift Hawk. You will see. You will see! You will see!*

Isabella, the oldest bloodhound, seven years old, half a year beyond the bloodhound's six-and-a-half-year life span, lay on a stretch of grassy ground, panting heavily. Her sides heaved out and back in as she struggled to breath, desperately rasping. Obviously, she was dying of bloat. Her pup, the Emperor, having been bitten multiple times by a water moccasin, was also in the throes of death. The two pit bulls had given up miles ago and were lost in the Florida like jungle.

The Rake, overcome with helplessness, was further petrified by the appearance of a great black dog who he thought to be two hundred pounds. As if he were an apparition, Rot was not there and then poof, he was there. He totally ignored Rake, as if he were of no consequence, in fact, not even there. Evidently, he had no fear of Jake nor did he seem to bear him any ill will. Both bloodhounds had been Rot's neighbors. He knew them though he had never been on the inside of their private fence. Going first to Isabella, who had never really been friendly toward him, he licked her in the face. She fixed her eyes upon him and, in dying, acknowledged his goodwill. Isabella then closed her eyes and was gone. Rot went to the Emperor and began to lick him in the face. He had been friendly toward Rot and responded with some moans of satisfaction. Rot continued to manifest a comforting presence. Before long, in a few minutes, the Emperor, too, closed his eyes, and he, too, was gone. Rot fixed his gaze upon the Rake. His eyes seem to light up and glare—blaze. Jake began to shake. Then Rot was gone—poof—he was no longer there.

Jake did not know what to do. He had nothing with which he could bury these great dogs. When had such a thing bothered anyone like Fitz! But it did stress out the Rake. He slept there that night beside the dogs, for the first time, mourning the death of two of God's creatures. In the morning, he walked out of the woods and called an Uber car. He would meet Fitz in St. Augustine, at Sonny's.

Meanwhile, Fitz was in the parking lot at a Sonny's in Saint Augustine. His red truck was at the far end of the lot where he hoped the black dog would not see it. Fitz sat in the cab of an animal patrol truck, talking to the driver. The animal patrol truck was parked near where one would enter Sonny's, next to the highway.

"As I was telling you," said Fitz, "this black dog, a rottweiler, is a vicious dog. He is a wild dog, a feral dog, like his vicious mother, the red dog, and he must be caught and eliminated."

"But I have some questions," said Getty, an animal control worker, a friend of Fitz and acquaintance from an earlier job enhancement meeting. "What did this black dog do? And how is it that you know he will be coming into this Sonny's parking lot? And how is it that you know it will be this morning? And why is it that you want me to release the dog to you? And even further, if this dog is so vicious and devious, how is it do you think we are going to catch him?"

"Too many questions," quipped Fitz. "Did you not listen to my story about how I killed the vicious red dog?"

"Yes," answered Getty.

"Did you not clap with the others?" chided Fitz.

"Yes," responded Getty.

"Did my promotion for such excellent service not put me in a rank above you?" bragged Fitz.

"Yes," Getty timidly replied.

"Wait! Look! There he is!"

"Where?" queried Getty.

"That big black dog over there at the entrance of the parking lot. He's looking right at us!"

It was Rot! And Rot stood rigid, eyes fastened on the animal control truck. "Stupid dog," said Fitz. Fitz, of course, had been walking around in the Sonny's parking lot. And Rot easily picked up his scent. It was unmistakable who he was! And Rot knew where he was.

Chapter 17

A Second Encounter

Rot did not move. He continued to stare at the truck. Fifteen minutes passed. Wolves stalk their prey sometimes waiting for hours before the appropriate time to leave their cover and strike. Fitz, of course, had little patience. Fifteen minutes equated to hours for him. Finally, Rot sat down. His concentration on the occupants of the animal control truck did not let up.

Another fifteen minutes passed. Getty had never seen a dog like this one. Most dogs did not have a clue that there was anyone such as animal control and that they were going to get you. If a dog had any concept of what animal control was about, the dog would flee, doing its best to avoid capture. Black dog was aware of what was happening and not only was he fully conscious of what was transpiring but he remained calm. Black dog seemed to think he was in control. It was like he knew Fitz was there and wanted him to be present. Did Black dog think he was the stalker instead of the stalked? Black dog's steadiness of purpose seemed phenomenal. His stare was challenging. It was like he had no place to go. Black dog was going nowhere nor did he advance toward them. It was like a stalemate.

Finally, at Fitz's urging, Getty got out of his animal control truck, Fitz slowly following hesitantly behind him. They slowly scuffed toward Rot. Rot came to his feet. Rot crouched like a pro linebacker, ready to spring into action. Getty could hear Fitz dragging his feet behind him. When they were halfway to Rot, Getty stopped. He continued looking at Rot but spoke to Fitz. "Fitz," he said, "this dog is not moving."

Rot continued to stare at the two, like he was looking right through them. "Fitz," he said, "this black dog is huge and fierce looking. I can see the muscles rippling in his shoulders and back legs. His neck is like a tree trunk. He is not showing his teeth, which I presume are viciously intimidating. I can see his tail is stiff, pointing toward the heavens. I can tell you right now, this dog is not one with which anyone should mess. I work with dogs all the time, but I am afraid of this dog. He is truly awesome."

Fitz suggested, "Call him and see if he will come."

"I don't know his name," said Getty.

"I think his name is Rot," said Fitz.

They were about twenty yards away.

"Here, Rot, here, Rot,'" said Getty.

There was no change in Rot's demeanor, but he did take a couple of steps toward them. So Getty and Fitz backed up a few steps. As Getty continued to beckon Rot forward, Getty and Fitz slowly went backward, moving ever closer to the animal control truck.

"See," said Fitz, "I told you he was a stupid dog."

Rot had never been called a stupid dog. He had seen at a dog park another dog berated by a neurotic owner who called his dog stupid. Rot understood what Fitz was saying. Even so, he continued forward. Fitz had made sure both he and Getty had cans of mace with them. As they came to the animal control truck, Fitz opened the back door and climbed into the truck. "What are you doing, Fitz?" inquired Getty.

"This stupid dog is following us. He will follow us right into the truck. We will both mace him at the count of three. A full blast in the face. He will fold, and we will have him. I have some specially made chains that I'll put on him, and I'll take him in my truck back to DeLand."

Getty said, "You must be crazy. Why get in the back of the truck? You think I'm going to get into the back of the truck with that dog? Especially with him in between us and the doorway?"

Fitz, like a broken record, repeated, "Don't you remember how I got that Red dog? If we try to mace that strong dog out here in the open air, he might get away. Inside the truck, in a closed-in area, we will ambush him, and he will not get away. It is a cinch. I'm telling you. He is a stupid dog."

"But we'll be in the truck, and he will have us trapped," argued Getty.

"Get in the back of the truck, and get your mace ready," commanded Fits.

Thus, Getty climbed in the back of the animal control truck, joining Fitz up tight against the steel mesh screen dividing between that section of the truck and the front seats. Getty's can of mace was ready. Rot had come right up to the rear of the truck, and it looked like he was going to respond to Getty's coaxing—jumping right into the truck.

However, with a swift movement, Rot positioned himself behind the open truck back door and slammed it shut. There was no inside knob on the door of this vehicle, no windows, and no access to the trucks front, since there was an immovable screen that separated animal passengers from animal control employees. To make matters worse, Fitz, like many years ago when he accidently and unconsciously had been thrust backward by El, Red's mother, and pulled his shotgun's trigger, injuring her, and with his second shot, killed the dog defending its puppies, now with a nervous reaction, pushed his mace can button, filling the back of the animal control truck with suffocating fumes. Getty and Fitz were choking and choking for an hour—floods of tears running down their cheeks from their eyes.

Rot followed a customer into Sonny's, and its owner/manager was delighted to renew acquaintances with the great dog. Rot was given a few chicken breasts minus the bones and some bowls of water. While Getty and Fits were berating each other for not having their cell phone available—Getty's being in front of the animal control vehicle, and Fits in his red truck—Rot was enjoying the air-conditioning of Sonny's and praises of numerous customers who recognized him as a dog of exceptional proportions and one of remarkable persona.

Not only were Getty and Fitz locked in a small confined space reeking foul mace fumes, but both were extremely hungry. Fitz now realized he had not eaten since breakfast the previous day. Not only was he hungry, but he now became aware that he was parched with thirst. It also occurred to him that his legs were red with horrendous irritation. He could not cease to scratch them. The poisonous ivy fluid with each successive series of scratching was running down numerous areas of his tormented legs.

Along with all this, relations between Getty and Fitz had not only deteriorated beyond repair, but Getty realized what a fraud Fitz was. Word would soon get out. Fitz's respect as a first-rate animal control employee would soon suffer damage beyond repair.

Meanwhile, Sonny's manager did not know where Rot's owner was or how Rot got to his place of business. He remembered when Preacher came by on his last trip, he was headed north, noting he was going to visit friends at Pope AFB in North Carolina. Not knowing how Rot had come to Augustine, and thinking his friend might be at Pope, since there was a trucker eating there that very morning who greatly admired Rot and was going right by the base, the Sonny restaurant owner arranged a ride with the trucker to deliver Rot to the base.

When the ride was explained to Rot, he seemed to understand. The words Pope AFB stood out in his mind. When he heard the words, he barked, like, "Yes, yes, that is where I want to go!" He knew where it was. Of course, it was off I-95, going north to Pennsylvania and on the way to Philacanes. Rot did not understand about road routes and such, but he did know about Pope AFB, and he knew where he was going. And Pope AFB was next in his mind. As he exited Sonny's, he noted Jake was letting Fitz and Getty out of the animal control truck. He barked to make sure they saw him get into the eighteen-wheeler. He was looking out the passenger window as the truck exited the parking lot and headed north on I-95.

Getty, telling Fitz to never call him again, left in the animal control truck. Fitz and the Rake got changes of clothes from their truck. This time, Fitz wore long-legged jeans to cover his emasculated legs. Both chowed down at Sonny's, and Fitz tactfully learned that "magnificent rottweiler," as he deceitfully called him to the Sonny's owner, was traveling to Pope AFB in North Carolina.

As they left Sonny's, Fitz said, "That Rot is a stupid dirty dog. I'll get him. Do you know what he did, Jake?"

"What?" Jake incredulously asked.

"He lured us in to the back of that animal control truck and locked us in it."

Jake was about to ask "How did he do that?" but he thought better of it.

"First," said Fitz, who was driving, "we've got to stop by a drugstore and get some calamine lotion. I think I picked up some poison ivy on my legs. Can't think of how I did that. Now tell me what happened with our chase using the bloodhounds."

The Rake responded, "They both died."

Fitz did not even care to ask how. It did not matter to him. "Right before they expired," Jake exclaimed, "the black dog came and licked them in the face."

"What!" thundered Fitz, leaning to the right and backhanding the Rake with a vicious blow to his head. "The black dog came, and you have a pistol, and you did not shoot him!"

"I couldn't do that," cried the Rake. "I knew you wanted to capture him and torture him before you killed him."

"Ah," said Fitz, "you finally did something right. Good thinking."

Jake, unable to resist, blurted out, "Emperor died a terrible death. He was bitten again and again by a water moccasin."

"A snake," muttered Fitz. "I hate snakes—all four kinds, little ones and big ones, live ones and dead ones. I hate snakes, even more than I hate that dog—Rot. Snakes, ugh." Fitz shivered. His whole body quivered as he spoke about them.

Chapter 18

The Truck Ride

In the truck traveling north, Rot sat on the passenger's side of the cab, and he focused his total persona on the driver intently observing him in deep thought. The driver, Chick, while keeping his eyes on the road ahead, kept looking to the right at Rot. "What is this dog thinking?" Chick muttered to himself. Chick, of course, talked kindly to Rot. He kept engaging in conversation as though he and Rot were the best of friends and had always been so.

"I like driving this truck," said Chick. "Our perspective from way up here on the seat is great. We can see far ahead of us, and we are quite safe. I also like the big mirrors on both sides of our cab. I can see what's on both sides of us and on behind us." To Chick's amazement, Rot looked to his right at the rearview mirror on his side of the truck. Rot seemed to nod his head.

Chick kept reflecting, *There is something familiar about this dog. What is it?* Finally, it dawned on him. *This dog reminds me of Teddy.* Teddy, of course, was a redbone and not a rot. What Chick had surmised earlier was that Teddy, his champion coon dog, was the father of Red (Rot's mother). Teddy was Rot's grandfather. Teddy and Red, Rot's mother, had been teamed together in coon-trials, and they were champions. In the scheme of events that occur in our lives, there is much that we do not know. It is like there is a Master-Planner who is always with us, directing us, looking out for us, and delivering us. Often, for example, we escape tragedy on a highway, and we think our continuance is based on our personal ability to persevere. The truth is, we were delivered by the invisible hand of a gracious and merciful Presence. In the life of El, Red, and Rot, it was only appropriate that Chick have a part in the Day of Rot. That is the way it is! Chick, of course, did not know Rot was the son of Red. Chick did not know what had happened to Red.

Rot, too, was quite comfortable with Chick. Chick, as was Preacher, was from Philacanes. Preacher and Chick knew each other and had hunted together. The atmosphere from which they had come made them kindred spirits as animal lovers. They were similar in spirit and the treatment of dogs. Rot picked it up immediately. Sometimes, animals are smarter than humans.

Stopping at Love's, where there were many other trucks, getting gas, as well as an assortment of vehicles with passengers gassing up, using the restrooms, buying various kinds of goods such as Subway sandwiches, Chick got some water for Rot and took him on a brief walk. Back at the truck, in the large adjacent parking lot with many other trucks, he was approached by a stocky six-foot man who pranced in a show-off short-stepped weight-lifter stride with a hunched back and swinging boastful arms swaying to the left and then right, and back and forth.

To the man's right sauntered a large brindle-red pit bull of awesome dimensions, a dog over one hundred pounds. Bull, as the man was called, was a friend of Fitz. His dog, Tog, had been scheduled to fight Killer. Fitz had called Bull, telling him about the rot who had destroyed Killer in a vicious surprise ambush. Fitz, not missing a trick, informed Bull that rot was traveling up Interstate 95 in an eighteen-wheeler. From seeing the departure of Rot in Chick's truck, Bull was given a description of the truck, its license number, and the dog, Rot. Bull, who lived in South Carolina, near south of the border, promised to delay Rot. Though Fitz wanted to cause trouble for Rot, he did not actually want Bull to destroy Rot. Fitz, for certain, wanted the pleasure of bringing about the demise of Rot himself with sadist pleasure.

Bull, however, not a person of emotional wellness and highly overrating his own sense of prowess as well as that of his dog, wasted no time but went immediately into an attack mode. Rot was not on a leash, and neither was Tog. Tog, of course, was trained to fight and had experienced success at it. Pointing at Rot, Bull said to Tog, "Sic, Tog. Sic. Get him!"

Some other truckers, evidently from the area conversing nearby, noted what appeared to be a developing contest with two large dogs. One remarked, "Look, it's TTT."

Another said, "What is a TTT?"

Someone replied, "Tog the Terrible."

The first prophesied, "That big black dog is in trouble. This may be his demise."

Preacher, conversing with a friend, had told him, "I'm training my dog, Rot, in what I call dog karate, martial arts."

His friend warned, "That's good for you and your dog, but in a contest with another dog, it won't matter."

Preacher replied, "You think?"

And his friend had answered, "I think!"

Chick was totally taken aback by Bull and Tog. He thought fighting your dog is extremely cruel. Why would you put your animal in a predicament where it got ripped apart, maybe crippled, and killed? And even if your dog won, why would you let it do serious injury to another? To do such was barbaric and savage. Nevertheless, such was unfolding before his eyes to the dog that had been committed into his care. Before he could do anything about it, Tog, a vicious ball of fury with snorts and growls, lunged forward, seeking to inflict on Rot, a dog he did not even know, horrendous bodily damage.

But surprise of surprises. How he did it? One could not comprehend. You could not explain it. You just had to see it. Rot was not there. Somehow, he ended up to his left of Tog, and with his back right leg, he swiped under the rear feet of Tog. Tog was flipped in the air, and Rot, with his body, gave him a hard thump, knocking him on his back with his legs flailing toward the sky. The air knocked out of him, Tog laid on the ground a full thirty seconds, while all the time, Bull was frantically yelling, "Tog, get him. Sic, sic, sic!"

Tog, recovered, was up. Tog, a smart dog, charged again, this time veering to the right to avoid the move Rot had just used on him, when he had evaded Tog by a lightning quick move to Tog's left. However, this time, Rot moved to the right. Again, Tog not even coming close to touching him. With his back left leg, he again swiped Tog's rear legs out from under him, and bumping him hard up into the air, this time slamming him to the ground with both front feet on Tog's chest. It took Tog a full minute to recover. Meanwhile, Bull was going bonkers. He had never seen such a thing.

This time, thought Tog, *I have him*. Once Tog got his vicious bulldog teeth into another dog, he would not let go, and it would mean serious bodily damage. This time, as Tog charged, Rot did not go to the left or the right but up and over. No matter how fast Rot was or deceptive if he went over Tog, Tog would only have to follow his movement and slightly raise his head to get his powerful jaws on Rot. But, again, Rot did something totally unexpected. When Tog opened his mouth to grab ahold of Rot, Rot rammed his right front leg into the mouth of Tog and right down his throat. Rot was larger than Tog by at least fifteen pounds, and he, too, was an amazingly strong dog. His weight, muscle, and leg choked Tog and smashed him to the ground this third time, cutting off his air. The fight went out of Tog.

Rot pulled his leg out of Tog's throat. Rot sat down in front of Tog, and Tog lay belly up in surrender, gasping for breath. Rot had defeated Tog with no injury to himself and really none to Tog. The onlooking truckers clapped.

Bull, horrified by seeing Tog present his belly to Rot, the sure sign of an omega to an alpha, the position of an inferior to the superior, took the leather leash off Tog that he had been carrying and started beating him for his submission.

Chick, eighteen-inch arms and large muscular hands from hard manual work, an exceptionally tough man, stepped forward, placing the thumb of his right hand under the chin of Bull, and the index fingers of the right hand, inside the lower lip of Bull, and exerted extreme pressure, pressing the thumb up and pulling down with his two fingers. If done viciously, a person's lower face can be pulled down under the chin. Nevertheless, such a move is horrendously painful to a person so incapacitated. Chick said slowly, distinctly, and forcefully, "Do not beat your dog." Chick repeated it three times.

Bull walked off. This time, without the pretense of his tough man strut. One of the onlooker truckers came forward and claimed Tog. Tog's new owner made it clear that he did not believe in dog fighting nor beating his animal.

Chick and Rot got back into Chick's truck. As they continued north on Interstate 95, they listened to country music, and Chick shared with Rot a bag of beef jerky. He loved beef jerky, and evidently, so did Rot. Chick would eat a piece, and then he would give Rot a piece. He kept looking at Rot, and of course, Rot was always looking at him. *I think*, thought Chick, *I see a smirk on Rot's face.* Chick said to Rot, over and over, "You are one smart dog."

So it was incredulous that a great dog only recently descended from a great white wolf would be so comfortable traveling with an unfamiliar man. Most visualize the family of the dog only recently descended from the wolf. Not realizing it was the dogs of Adam out of paradise lost that became the wolf. Now here, slightly before the wolf returns to dwell with the lamb, it is visualized in Rot what has been inherent in the wolf and the animal world all along.

Chapter 19
Pope AFB

Chick, following his GPS, exited Interstate 95, and soon, he and Rot were at the main entrance of Pope AFB. Pulling his large rig off to the right, he parked where delivery vehicles stopped to acquire entrance to the base. Two SPs, security police, were on duty, and one, a woman SP came over to Chick's truck to inquire about his intention.

"I have a dog," said Chick, "that I have been asked to deliver to this base."

"Yes," said the SP, "our base commander has been expecting you. I'll call him, and he should be here in just a few minutes."

It had only been recently that Preacher and Rot had journeyed north from Deland to Pennsylvania along this same route. His friend in St. Augustine, remembering Preacher and Rot's visit, had assumed Rot was following the same route and had packed him off to Pope AFB with a truck driver, namely Chick. The Sonny's owner had called Preacher, on second thought, and informed him of his dog's whereabouts. Preacher had called a friend in Fayetteville who he had visited. The friend, Steve Mack, had been part of a youth group Preacher had supervised years earlier when he was a chaplain at Pope AFB. Steve was a good friend of the base commander and had asked him to intercept Rot and hold him until he could pick Rot up.

In a matter of three or four minutes, a blue air force car with a white eagle on a blue flag on it appeared—meaning it was the base commander's vehicle. The car came out the base exit, did a U-turn, and pulled up behind Chick's truck. A tall man with a hat with white clouds and lightning bolts on its beak and silver eagles on his shirt lapels exited the car and strove forward. Chick got out of the truck, followed by Rot, and stood at attention. He raised his right hand slanted to his forehead, just above his right eye. Rot stood to his right and raised his right paw in the same slanted position, just above his right eye.

The colonel raised his hand in a slant above his right eye, in a crisp AF salute, and then dropped his hand. He then said, "At ease."

Then Chick dropped his right hand, and Rot dropped his right paw and sat. All this, of course, was not necessary. Chick did not have to salute the colonel since he was a civilian, nor did the colonel expect him to do so.

The colonel's first words were, "I'm really impressed with this dog. Obviously, he is a military dog. His owner, I understand, used to be a chaplain on this base. He had what was called the God Patrol and used to drive around in a Volkswagen painted like a C-130 airplane. His friend, Steve Mack, told me all about it. There are a few other people who live in our area who still remember it."

Chick put his right hand on his chin and pondered for a minute. Then he said, "I know that chaplain. He's from the same town I'm from in Pennsylvania—Philacanes."

"Well," said the colonel, putting out his right hand, "I'm Chuck, the commander of Pope AFB."

Chick extended his right hand, and they shook as he said, "I'm Chick Johnston and was asked to deliver this dog, Rot, to Pope AFB."

Rot made a low whining sound while standing and extending his right paw.

The colonel bent down and shook his paw, saying, "I'm glad to meet you, Rot."

Rot gave two low sounding barks in response.

At that time, two other vehicles pulled up both behind the colonel's car. The first was a Fayetteville Animal Control truck, and the second was a red four-door pickup. Out of the animal control truck exited Steve Mack, stopping to salute the colonel as he approached. Following proper greetings between the colonel and Steve, Steve introduced himself to Chick and thanked him for delivering Rot.

Rot and Steve had a joyous greeting, at which time Steve gave Rot some enthusiastic petting, which was followed by the same from Colonel Chuck.

The small enclave of goodwill was rudely interrupted by the three occupants of the red truck. Not saluting or even giving a greeting or introduction, which is extremely impolite in a military setting, came Fitz boldly asserting, "I have come for that black dog. He is wanted in DeLand, Florida."

Nobody, of course, talks down to a base commander on his own base. They were not really on Pope AFB, but the entranceway was considered part of the base property. The base commander, stepping in front of Fitz, said, "For what is he wanted?"

Fitz inserted, "That's my business."

"Not on my base," replied the commander. "What happens here is my business."

Steve Mack, speaking from the rear of Fitz, said, "Fitz showed up at my office, showing identification from Florida as an employee of animal control and had heard Rot was being delivered to Pope AFB. But Fitz, you have no authorization here. This is North Carolina, and we don't extradite dogs to other states."

Bull, having met with Fitz and informing him of Tog's demise, now accompanying Fitz and Jake, broke into the conversation stating that Rot was a fighting dog and had killed his dog, Tog, just a few hours ago, just south of the border. Rot lay down, his head on his extended front legs, hearing his name referred to again and again, knowing he had friends present and would be dealt with fairly. He was not one to run away nor was he afraid.

Chick now entered the conversation. He said, "I know Rot's owner, and he is 100 percent against dogfighting. In fact, Rot was with me at a Love's truck stop, and this man called Bull, trying to get a dogfight going, commanded his dog, Tog, to attack Rot. Rot soundly defeated Tog without hurting him. He never even bit Tog. Then this man, Bull, beat his dog. And he also walked off, deserting Tog."

The base commander said, "Loves is south of the border in South Carolina. Again, you all have no authority here."

ROT

By now, the group had drawn up into a half circle, all surrounding Rot, the center of all conversation and attention. Rot knew who Fitz was and glared intensely at him. Through it all, low growls seeped from his lips. His size, demeanor, body language, and teeth, if he exposed them, were totally awesome. But he was wise beyond normal human perception, so he kept his pose, trusting in those present who he believed would fairly represent him.

Fitz, now losing all composure, jettisoning his normal successful persuasive trait of deception, shouted, "Well, this killer dog killed my dog, Killer!"

Chuck, the base commander remarked, "Did you accuse Rot of being a killer? And did you say your dog was called Killer?"

A bewildered look manifested itself on Fitz's face.

"I know who you are, Fitz," quipped Chick. "You killed Philacanes' famous hunting dog, El. You shot her with a sixteen-gauge shotgun and killed all her pups, except a dog named Red."

For the first time, Fitz recognized Chick. He remembered the conversation from long ago in Mason's bar and Chick's statement that it would not go well with anyone who harmed El.

Jake the Rake, who had remained silent through this whole conversation, had his eyes open for the first time. "And Fitz killed this dog's mother, Red, and all her puppies," said the Rake. "He falsely claimed it was his duty as an employee of animal control. It's Fitz that is into dog fighting."

At Jake's comment, Fitz lost it all. He lunged forward with a tremendous right-handed haymaker, hitting his partner right in the nose. Blood spurted from Jake right on the neatly pressed uniform of the base commander who was standing to the left of Fitz and Jake. Orders were swift. The woman SP, who was standing nearby, off to the left, was ordered to handcuff Fitz and put him into base confinement.

Fitz protested, "You can't do this! I'm not in the air force."

However, he was at the gate of this base. He had bloodied the uniform of an air force colonel—the base commander. And Fitz was guilty of assault and battery. He was locked up.

The base commander went home to change his clothes. Chick now realized Rot was the son of Red. Glad that he had met Rot, he left in his truck to head north on I-95. Steve, with Rot, took Jake to a local hospital. Bull drove off in Fitz's red truck. Rot, having been a bystander in all this, spent the rest of the day with a smirk on his face. He knew where he was going, what he would do, and had an innate assurance that all would go as he envisioned.

Chapter 20

Rot's New Friend

Jake had a broken nose. He broke with Fitz and, being miles away from home, had nowhere to go. Steve took him home with Rot. Rot was to wait for a friend of Preacher's brother to pick him up and take him on to Pennsylvania. Jake was welcomed by Steve's family. Rot, having been in the home of Steve recently, was welcomed by the entire family: Steve and his wife, Lola, and their three children, Elijah, Tamar, and Ruth.

Rot ignored Jake. He knew Jake killed Red, his mother, and had been with Fitz, seeking to do him harm. Rot did not seek to bite Jake. He did not growl at him. Rot did, though, keep away from him. Jake was afraid of Rot and kept far away from him while being in the same house.

The next morning, the whole family, including Jake and Rot, went to church. It was unusual for a dog to go to church, but one family had a service dog, which sat near his master, an 82d vet who had lost his legs. Rot sat in the aisle, near the chair of Lola, simulating the behavior of the Belgium shepherd two rows ahead. The shepherd knew Rot was there, and he knew the shepherd was there. Neither dog bothered the other.

Steve was the guest preacher this Sunday, since the regular pastor of this church was away. After an inspirational song service and communion, Steve stood before the congregation on the slightly elevated platform and read his text for that morning, John 3:1–15. Like George Whitefield thundered, along the eastern coast of the thirteen colonies, just before the American Revolution in a great revival, "You must be born again," so Steve in his bass voice sounded, "You must be born again."

Jake, sitting four seats to the right of Lola, snapped to attention. His entire persona focused on Steve and the message. Steve explained, "To go to heaven, one must be born of the Spirit. You must become a new person. Only God can give *Zoe* (a special Greek word for life) to an individual. The good news is one can have a new life, a spiritual life, and all our sin can be forgiven."

At one point, Steve said, "Just as Moses lifted up the serpent in the wildness, even so the Son of man had to be lifted up, that whosoever believes in Him should not perish but have eternal life" (John 3:14–15 MEV). Steve explained when the people of Israel on their wilderness journey spoke against God, God sent poisonous serpents that bit them, and they, of course, died. When the people repented and asked Moses to pray for them, Moses had them make a bronze serpent and put it on a pole. When people who were bitten looked at the bronze serpent, they lived (Numbers 21:4–9).

So Jesus taught, when he was crucified, people bitten by the serpent, which includes everyone, were to look to Him by faith to receive the forgiveness of their sin and to live. This wilderness experience of Israel was to teach us today about salvation.

Moses, who wrote the first five books of the Bible (Deuteronomy 31:24) had written Genesis 3:15, which is the first of a long line of prophecy concerning the promise of Jesus Christ as our Savior. In this verse, God addresses the serpent, namely Satan, and the woman, Eve, who ate of the fruit of the tree of the knowledge of good and evil and gave of this fruit to her husband, Adam. God said there would be enmity between the people who belonged to Satan and to those who were the offspring of the woman—those God had birthed to be His people, the sons of God. In the prophecy given by God, it was said, "He will bruise your head." That meant He, the one born of a woman of God's choosing, namely Mary—Jesus would destroy the serpent, Satan, by tromping on his head. And Satan, the serpent, would bruise his heel. Satan, like a poisonous snake that bites one on the heel as they walked by, would affect all humans with death. "For the wages of sin is death, but the gift of God is eternal life through Jesus our Lord" (Romans 6:23).

Those bitten by the serpents in the Old Testament account were to recognize that Satan had given them death. They were bitten on the heel. At the same time, looking at the bronze serpent they were indicating in the future, according to the prophecy of Genesis 3:15, they would be healed through the bruising of the serpent, crushing of his head. Jesus, the Son of God, God born in the flesh, without sin, dying for us, taking our punishment on the cross, would defeat Satan and give us eternal life. Jesus came to destroy the devil and the power he had over us in death (Hebrews 2:14).

So Jesus indicated we are to look at Him on the cross and see the fulfillment of Genesis 3:15. Like people in the Old Testament were healed by looking prophetically to the bruising of the serpent, so we are healed by having our sin transferred to Jesus, and Him dying as our substitute. Steve accented, "Jesus said, 'And I, if I am lifted up from the earth, will draw all people to Myself'" (John 12:32 NKJV).

Steve wrapped it up by announcing, "You must be born again—John 3:3. You must be born of the water and the Spirit—John 3:5. Jesus invites, 'Come to Me, all you who labor and are heavy laden, and I will give you rest'—Matthew 11:28."

The congregation was asked to stand, and those who wanted to be saved were invited forward as they sang "Just as I Am, Without One Plea." The first stanza was "Just as I am, without one plea, but that thy blood was shed for me, and that thou bidd'st me come to Thee, O Lamb of God, I come, I come."

There was a stirring to the right of Rot. Jake was rapidly making his way in front of those standing to his left. Rot, sensing Jake's movement, repositioned to let Jake pass. Down the aisle, swiftly came Jake, almost at a run. Steve received Jake and asked him, while the congregation continued to sing, why he had come. Jake said, "I come to receive Jesus as my Savior and to ask God to give me the new birth."

When the congregation finished the invitation, Steve asked everyone to be seated.

Jake asked Steve, "May I say something?"

Steve answered, "Of course," giving Jake the mike.

Jake said, "My life is a mess. My job is in DeLand, Florida, but I am not going back there. I have no family, and the one person who I really trusted I have come to see is a mean man without principles. I joined him in dog fighting and have been deeply troubled by images of the dogs we have viciously killed and left physically damaged, too horrible for you to visualize. I have trouble sleeping at night. And the dog I regret killing the most is Red dog."

At that, Rot's head snapped up. He recognized Jake was talking about his mother.

"That dog there, Rot"—he pointed at Rot, and Rot knew it—"is the son of Red dog, a famous dog from Philacanes, Pennsylvania. Rot," Jake said, "I ask your forgiveness."

Rot was looking right at Jake, intensely. Jake continued, "I have been studying this for some time. Rot is probably the son of the large rottweiler Fitz's dog killed while we were training dogs to fight in the Ocala National Forest. My friend, Fitz, who killed Red's mother, El, and who, along with me, killed Red, is trying to kill Rot. But something is happening. I don't know what, but God is using this great dog, Rot, for some special purpose."

Jake was speaking much longer than usual, but the congregation found what was happening here this morning amazing. Jake noted Rot was part wolf. "A wolf," said Jake, "is a dog gone wild through corruption brought on by Satan. Yet the wolf is not evil but waiting to return to the sheep—for as I heard Billy Graham say, 'The wolf will lay down with the lamb' (Isaiah 11:6).

"God, I have found, does not want us to be wolves but tells us we are sheep—I see this in the twenty-third Psalm. Red ran with wolves. Rot walks with the sheep. Wolves are smarter than humans. Wolves spend their whole life trying to survive. Humans want to control and destroy. Fitz, my past associate, wants only to hurt and kill. Rot is smarter than Fitz. Rot will do what he does God's way. The meek will inherit the earth. Rot will prevail over Fitz. This morning, I am separating myself from Fitz. I choose God's way. I have accepted the invitation of Jesus Christ. I surrender myself to you, Lord Jesus

Christ. Forgive me of my sin through your precious blood. Give me, I ask, a new birth. My greatest desire is to be a Christian."

After the church service and a noon meal at a local restaurant where Rot was welcome along with the service dog of the hero from the 82d, Steve and his family, plus numerous others, gathered at a heated swimming pool of one of the church members. After some singing, Steve and Jake entered the pool, both having been furnished swimming trunks by the pool owner. Steve, with his left hand holding on to Jake's right hand, said, "Do you, Jake, believe that Jesus is the Son of God, the Christ, meaning King? And do you place your trust in Him as your Savior?"

Jake answered, "I do!"

Then Steve said, as he placed his right hand behind Jake's head, and immersed him beneath the water, "Buried with Christ in the likeness of His death, raised by Christ to walk in newness of life."

Those along the poolside sang, "Now I belong to Jesus, Jesus belongs to me, not for the years of time along, but for eternity."

Jake was weeping profusely. Many of the bystanders were crying. As Jake came to the side of the pool, there was Rot. Rot was an awesome dog, only 125 pounds but horrendously fearsome. Jake moved slowly, not quite sure what was going to happen. Being six-foot-three, he came to the part of the pool where he was in five feet of water. As the top part of his body appeared poolside and his arms rested over the side of the pool, Rot drew nigh. *What?* thought Jake. And so did everyone else! Rot, approaching slowly, looking steadfastly into Jack's face, eyeball-to-eyeball, hesitated momentarily, as would an alpha of considerable personality, then licked Jake in the face. In fact, he did so three times. In seconds, it was all over as quickly as it had begun. "What an incredible dog," said Steve.

Rot's action declared, "Jake, you are forgiven. You are now my friend."

It meant a great deal to Jake!

The pool owner's two labs then jumped into the pool. Labs love the water. Rot, not adapted to swimming, joined them as did the service dog of the vet from the 82d. Everyone was joyous, and all had a good time. They were joined by Heck, sent by the brother of Preacher, and others. Many stayed for hamburgers and hotdogs plus other delicacies. Meanwhile, Fitz remained incarcerated at Pope AFB, stewing in his own juices.

Chapter 21
Rot Takes to the Air

Rot knew exactly what he was doing. Wolves are patient but persistent. The part of his character related to the characteristic of a wolf did not cause him to act foolishly. He was headed to a definite locale with a specific goal. It, however, would take him a lot longer and be much more difficult if he made his way traveling by foot across the terrain between Florida and Pennsylvania to accomplish his purpose. He had traveled this route recently, and he knew where he wanted to go. As it happened, he found himself on his way to fulfill the plan that had been planted in his mind. Rot was relaxed, not unreasonably anxious. He pressed on, knowing at the appropriate moment, he would act. Like his mother, Red, when dognapped, he would press on and seize the point of time, for which he strove when it arrived. He seemed to know that it would come.

Monday morning, Jake went to work with Steve. Steve was the director of animal control in Fayetteville. He thought he could get Jake employment there. Steve would see to it that Jake had found living quarters, and he would assist Jake until he could get established.

In the meantime, Fitz had been released from his incarceration at Pope AFB. He was guilty of an attack on his friend, assault and battery, but the AF did not have the authority to try civilians for criminal activity. He learned the dog, Rot, had been passed on to a person called "Heck" who was at Fort Bragg to pick up a helicopter and fly it back to the armory in Kingston, Pennsylvania. So Fitz, having located his red pickup truck, now alone, was on his way to Fort Bragg to get Rot.

Heck, meeting with the vet called Chief from Fort Bragg, joined with him and his dog, Warrior, at the war dog training center. Rot, larger than most of these dogs, was admired by numerous trainers. Heck, quite familiar with the dogs and their training, wanted to see what Rot could do with one of the exercises. After watching a few dogs execute going over a rope, simulating as crossing from one side of a cliff to the other, the dog traveling upside down, moving along, paw over paw, which was an amazing feat, Rot observing as well, Heck asked if Rot could try it. Remember, Rot had been trained to do all kinds of such feats from a puppy. When directed to the rope and commanded to cross, Rot went up on the Rope and traversed upside down, paw over paw, front legs and back, until he had gone down the robe from one end to the other. He then skillfully turned around and came back. The trainers were amazed. "This dog saw the rope feat one time, and he skillfully performed it successfully. The dog you call Rot is fantastically skilled and intelligent."

Heck inserted, "I've heard this dog is skilled in martial arts."

One of the trainers requested Heck give a demonstration. Heck explained to Rot, "We are going to do some martial arts." He had already established a friendly relationship with Rot, so sensing his attitude, Rot was not threatened. Heck kicked out at Rot a few times, and each time, Rot skillfully moved to the left or the right. Heck said, "This dog is going to be hard to kick." He also noted that while going to the left or right, Rot hung right in there, not moving away or retreating.

This friendly sharing was interrupted by a rude interference from behind them. All the trainers and personnel in their facility, hearing about Rot and Heck, had gathered to see Rot the dog brought to the compound by Heck. Heck, surprised at the arrival of the personage of Fitz, was astounded that he had found them and had made his way into this center. Heck had heard about Fitz but had not met him. "Give me a go at it," said Fitz. "I'll show you how to kick the crap out of him."

Heck, who seemed to know something about this, said, "Have at it."

Fitz, to be sure, was way over his head. The truth was that Fitz was deathly afraid of Rot. Fitz, however, came forward. Rot for sure knew who he was. Approaching to a few feet in front of Rot, he carefully aimed a kick and viciously thrust his right foot forward to kick Rot in the face. Rot skillfully moved easily, avoiding contact. Not only that, he caught Fitz's foot and dumped him. Fitz angrily got up and tried again. This time with his left foot, and Rot adeptly dumped him again. Heck, Chief, and all the instructors were convulsed with laughter.

Fitz, rising again, said, "You must be Heck. Instead of the dog, I think I'll kick the crap out of you."

At this, Chief and the instructors and other dog personnel laughed even harder. "Obviously," said Chief, "you don't know who Heck is."

"Who is he?" inquired Fitz.

"Let's just put it this way," said another dog warrior, "Heck wrote the martial arts manual for the army. He has his seventh-degree black belt in Tae Kwon Do. You can't even touch this dog. What do you think Heck will do to you?"

Fitz looked at Heck. He had not really studied him. Now he began to study Heck. He noticed Heck was perfectly at ease, calm. He also saw the bodily presence of Heck, the way he carried himself, his facial expression and, for the first time, he was really filled with fear. Heck could easily dispense him with one quick move.

Fitz said not another word. He left in a hurry. He simply got out of there. He muttered under his breath, "Black dog, I'll catch you in Philacanes. And then we'll see what happens!"

Rot knew what was up. Yes, he knew. *We will meet again, and soon.*

In the meantime, Rot was with Heck. Heck was from Philacanes, eight years younger than Preacher, and he was the friend of Preacher's brother, Charles. He had grown up across Route 309 from Preacher's home, about two hundred yards away. In a family not having much economically, he spent a great amount of his time traversing the same forest in which Preacher spent a good deal of time. Following high school, Heck entered the army and was soon a ranger. It was amusing when the training instructors sought to train Heck how to make it in the wilderness because he knew more than most of them.

He was soon given permission to work on martial arts seven days a week, which he did passionately twelve hours a day. He wrote a martial arts manual for the army. Soon, he was in Delta Force, where eventually, he became a helicopter pilot, and there, like in everything, he excelled, probably because in everything he did, he applied himself fervently. Heck served in Vietnam.

The Christian grandmother of Heck who raised him, had a tremendous effect on his life. Preacher remembered in Sunday school when she got an attendance pin for not missing a day in twenty-five years. Who knows? Maybe it was because of her prayers that Preacher became a preacher.

In the army, Heck got a college degree, a master's degree, and a doctor of education. He became the dean of a college in Florida, but because of his expertise with helicopters, he finally gave in to government demands for his services and made himself available as a troubleshooter for military operations. When Preacher called his brother about the need to have Rot picked up at Pope AFB and transported to the Philacanes area of Pennsylvania, his brother knew Heck was going to Fort Bragg to pick up a helicopter and deliver it to their area. So he asked Heck to pick up Rot. Heck agreed to do so.

Heck was a remarkable character. He did not smoke, drink, or curse, sang in a church choir, and had a youth group in which he taught martial arts. Heck had one requirement for membership in martial arts. The young people had to have at least a C average in school. Heck really believed in education and sought to teach young people to take care of their educational needs.

So it was that Rot accompanied Heck to his assigned helicopter. Rot was buckled up, and after he was secure, they took off. It was a small helicopter, so Rot's view as they flew was spectacular. Sometimes Heck flew low so Rot could enjoy the landscape. Rot saw lots of cows, and often, he saw dogs, which were always interesting to him. Dogs seem to take notice of other dogs. There were plenty of people. Sometimes they waved. Rot, too, was interested in people.

The Interstate, which they followed considerably, also fascinated him, the various and sundry kinds of vehicles, especially the long seemingly trains of trucks. The lay of the land was significant—the forests that were interspersed along the highway and especially the mountains of Pennsylvania off to the east of Harrisburg and beyond. Rot kept a mental picture of it all, and it was especially glamourizing to a dog that was part wolf. A wolf would study the landscape and want to explore it with great excitement. The trip was a treat that Rot would always treasure.

Along the way, Heck talked to him like he was a combat dog on a special mission. Heck undoubtedly was a friend, a likable sort, one with who Rot felt comfortable and safe. It was a matter of hours, and as they neared their goal, Heck, to further test the copter, flew a little beyond Kingston, over Philacanes. Heck went low. Rot saw the house and barn with the wagon wheel just above Preacher's family residence. Circling around to the west, Rot saw the homeland of his mother's family, the wolves, and somewhat to the north, the destination he knew about and would soon seek. In the circling, they flew over Heck's friend's house, the brother of Preacher. Rot saw it all from the air. Heck, too, was telling him in detail about it. Rot, like Heck, when he set his mind to something, gave it his full attention. He, of course, with his wolf nature, had a clear memory of where he was going. In the copter, he saw it with his own eyes—with Heck—all from the air. Rot did not know the words, but his feeling was God is good. Praise the Lord.

Chapter 22

Mission Accomplished

Heck circled over the Kingston Armory. Rot, looking below, saw the red Ram truck of Preacher's brother. He barked excitedly three times. "Yea," said Heck, "there's my buddy." Rot could see Charles waving from below.

They were soon on the ground. Rot ran toward Preacher's brother. He did not jump on his leg. Rot was taught not to do that. Instead, he stopped in front of him and put out his right paw for a shake. After the shake, standing, tail wagging vigorously, Rot accepted a few pets from Charles.

Charles and Heck talked for a few minutes with Charles thanking Heck for delivering Preacher's dog. Heck walked over to Rot and bent over to talk to him. "You are one cool dog," said the Delta Force man. "You would make an outstanding war dog. I would be glad to have you as my sidekick in any battle."

Rot responded by licking Heck in the face. They shook, Heck extending his right hand, and Rot his right paw. Rot saluted. Heck returned his salute, and they parted.

Charles left Kingston on Route 309, which went right through Philacanes. Charles, of course, lived at the east end of Harvey's Lake—a lake with crystal clear water fed by a spring. It had been carved out by a glacier many years ago and was presently a resort area surrounded by many homes and businesses. Charles could have turned left going through the town of Dallas, traveling on to his residence by the Lake Road. Instead, he followed 309 north, entering Philacanes, going toward the home of his parents where he and Preacher had been reared. Rot recognized the land, including the area from which Red had come.

Turning left, leaving 309, going by Preacher's place, Charles continued west, toward his home. As they approached the road to Beaumont on which the birthplace of Red was located, Rot, sitting in the pickup's passenger side, barked, pointing with his right paw. So Charles turned right and, guessing what Rot wanted, pulled off the road in front of an old brown house. Rot wanted out, so Charles stopped the truck and walked around the front, letting him out. Rot turned right and ran down from the house to the old barn with a wagon wheel against its south side. The door by the wagon wheel was open, and Rot went inside the barn. No one lived on this property any longer and no one was around. In a few minutes, Rot emerged from the barn and wanted back in the Ram truck. Charles and Rot then proceeded to Harvey's Lake.

Charles knew Rot had something in mind, but he did not know what it was. That is why he went through Philacanes. The phones in Philacanes had been buzzing. Word of Chick's ride with Rot and the pursuit of Rot by Fitz had spread throughout the town. News of Red's death had spread to every home. Chick gave a description of Rot, and folks thought a showdown was imminent between Rot, son of Red, and Fitz. Both seemed to be headed north to Philacanes. Rogan, the owner of Red, had said to Fitz earlier, "Come to Philacanes, and you'll get what you deserve."

Barb, Charles' wife, had a big hug for Rot and made a big fuss over him. After greetings and a few licks from Rot, the three of them went to the family's main boathouse, got into the family's new boat used for water skiing and other activities, and rode to the far end of the nine miles around the beautiful body of water, to the Grotto, a restaurant famous for its pizza and other Italian food.

At the Grotto docks, Charles parked his boat, and the three went into the local gathering place. As usual, there were numerous people from Philacanes. As soon as they arrived and were seated, people began to gather. Dr. Renselar Skyler happened to be present. Coming over to Rot, she got down on her knees, weeping. She put her arms around him, hugged him, and kissed him on the face, she said, "Rot, I am so sorry about your mother, Red. She was such a fantastic dog. Red saved my life. I don't know what you're about, but may God bless you in it!" Rot licked Dr. Skyler in the face.

Hearing the word *Red* repeatedly, Rot seemed to comprehend. Many photos were taken, and unbelievably, Rot's photo was in the area morning paper. The line relating to the photo and article on Rot read "Rot, Son of Red, Returns to Philacanes."

Yes, Rot enjoyed his pizza. The next morning, Rot, having slept on the rug in front of the large family fireplace in the great room overlooking the lake, at 6:00 a.m., at the back door of the house, wanted out. Charles let him out and watched as he darted into the wooded area at the rear of his house, into a great field of a wealthy neighbor who owned the great preserve inhabited by Silver Wolf and his pack. Rot, running north for some distance, then turned east into the great preserve, loping toward Philacanes. The wolf in Rot took over his total being, possessing him, unleashing pent-up energy, passion, heretofore never experienced. The cunning of his mother, Red dog, flowed in his veins, and the prowess of the great white propelled him forward.

Inside the great preserve, Rot had only gone a few miles when he heard a howl. He paused. There it was again. In his mind's eye, Rot saw the Great Silver. Rot had never done so before, but he stopped and raised his nose to the heavens. Rot let out a perfect elongate howl as though he had been a wolf all his life. Red dog could have done no better. Then Rot, listening, heard many howls to the northeast. The woods were full of wolves. Rot could not see them. But they were there. They knew. And Rot knew. It was the Day of Rot.

On Rot loped till he went down through a dip, on the edge of a forest line to a blacktopped road. There he saw the old gray house, the dwelling of his mother, Red, in her early life, and the old gray barn sitting a little further northeast. In the driveway in front of the house was a red pickup truck. Rot, now with a brisk walk, stalked to the north of the barn, went down along its back side, at the east end of the barn, bypassed the barn's lower end, going south, rounding the end of the barn, started slowly west, the direction from which he had come. As on the day before, the side door to the barn hung open.

It was the door long ago through which one entered to feed the horses. It was the door that led to the area where El had had her pups. It was the door that Fitz had entered some years earlier to kill El and her pups. It was the door through which Rot would now enter. Silently, his padded feet moved in sure slow steps. Rot's nose told him what he wanted to know. Fitz was only a few feet away. His scent was easy to detect, especially since it had been some time since he had bathed. Fitz's body, as his spirit, stunk.

Entering the door with superb stealth, inch by inch, Rot stood about ten feet in front of Fitz. Fitz had found an old wooden chair and, worn out from his pursuit of Rot and the draining emotional fury of his hate, was sitting fast asleep, hunkered down in the chair with the back of his head against the inside west barn wall. Straddled across his lap was his sixteengauge shotgun—the same one used to kill El and her pups. It was the intention of Fitz to shoot Rot in the legs, as he had shot the back legs of El, and to slowly torture him by shooting various body parts, one after the other, until finally, he was dead. Then after exulting over his masterpiece of torture, like with El, he would throw Rot's pellet-ridden body into the waters of Bowman's Creek.

Rot made not a sound. He identified with Fitz in only one way. That is, he was going to get the maximum benefit out of giving to Fitz what he had coming to him. So Rot sat down and let Fitz sleep. Gradually, Fitz began to yawn. He started to sluggishly stir. Eventually, his eyes opened and began to focus. To Fitz, it was like he was having a nightmare. Shockingly, there, directly in front of him, sat Rot.

For a minute, which is a long time in such a torturous moment of realization, Fitz made no movement. Then he leaped into action, grasping for his shotgun with amazing speed, seeking to bring the barrel up—aiming at Rot and blasting away his hind legs. Rot, even quicker than Fitz, lunged forward, hitting Fitz in the chest with his front feet and smashing him back against the barn wall. There was a difference in what happened between Fitz and El and Fitz and Rot.

With El, Fitz had managed to get a shot off, which through no skill of Fitz, had incapacitated El's hind legs. With Rot, Fitz had not got a shot off, and Rot had snatched the shotgun out of Fitz's hands with his great powerful jaws. El had knocked Fitz back, but Rot had crushed him against the barn wall completely, knocking the wind out of him.

Rot just sat there with the shotgun in his jaws, tantalizing Fitz, who was trying to get his breath back and in total fear. Finally, Fitz got his wind, and overcoming his fear through his hate, as he had done with Red, he pulled his sidearm with which he could have shot Rot. But he did not want Rot to get off that easy. He wanted to blow Rot apart with his shotgun. Rot seemed to understand. Out the barn door, Rot went with the shotgun. Rot moved west up to the blacktopped road. Fitz followed. "That gun is heavy," said Fitz. "Soon, you'll drop it, and then I'll get it. You are a stupid dog. You don't even know enough to run away. When I get my gun, I'm going to blow you to pieces."

Across the road went Rot. Across the road went Fitz. Up the bank, into the great fields, to the west went Rot, stopping and looking back. Into the great fields went Fitz, cursing and hollering at Rot. Up the tree line went Rot, stopping and encouraging Fitz to follow. Up the tree line went Fitz. Down into a dip and up to the top of the other side went Rot, stopping, watching, and laying down the gun. Moving on hastily to get the gun, Fitz followed. Picking the gun up again, Rot moved west, repeating this procedure with some variation. Fitz continued telling Rot all the time, what a stupid animal he was. Fitz, who had read the early morning edition of the newspaper, repeated over and over, "How does such a stupid dog as you get his photo in the newspaper?"

Fitz soon became tired. His fat legs were not used to this kind of jaunt. But he yelled, again and again, "Soon, you will tire, stupid dog. And I'll get the gun. That'll be your undoing. I'm not even going to drag you back to Bowman's Creek. I'm going to leave your body for the vultures. You are like El—stupid. You are like Red—stupid. Stupid, stupid, Rot. That's you—a big dog with a little brain."

Fitz hardly noticed that the terrain they were traversing had somewhat changed. There were large rocks to the north, and the path they trod was bordered on the west by a good-sized creek. They walked on the path, east of the creek, to which Fitz gave no consideration. Ahead was a large flat rock at least fifty feet across going north and about twenty feet east to west. Rot had followed the path along the creek north, and about ten feet from the north end of the flat rock and right in the middle from east to west, he stopped. Turning so that he was facing Fitz, Rot laid Fitz's gun down. He then returned south, about ten feet away from the gun. Rot then turned facing east, away from Fitz and the shotgun, and he laid down. He laid there, panting as though he could go no further. How convenient for Fitz! Fitz thought nothing of it. Fitz thought Rot was a stupid dog.

Fitz said, "Well, it's about time. I knew you were a stupid dog. Now I'm going to give you what you deserve." Fitz hastily moved north along the creek in an arc to the left of Rot and around him to retrieve his shotgun. Fitz, his mind only on one thing, and that was blowing large holes of double-ought steel balls into the body of Rot, tearing it apart, failed to notice off the great rock, at its north end, was a large crevice running into the great rocks. Fitz circled to the left of Rot and maneuvered himself behind Rot to avoid him.

As he approached his shotgun to bend over and pick it up, Rot, knowing where he was by sound and smell, came alive, quickly turned, and lunged toward him. Rot, of course, did not push Fitz, nor did he even touch him. In shock and fear, Fitz stumbled backward from where Rot had positioned him, across and off the north edge of the great rock. Off the rock, the loose ground underneath him crumbled, and he cascaded downward, some ten feet into a large pit, which ran the width of the large flat rock, some twenty feet. The back end of the pit formed a den, which faced southeast.

The large fissure just before the great rocks had dirt in it but was itself mostly rock with numerous stones in the wall unto which one or something could use to crawl to the surface above. Fitz, free-falling from above, thumped unto the crevice bottom, rolling over and over against and among many other bodies, which the sudden and violent impact of his fall had stirred. There was life in this pit, and Fitz, rolling around in it and partially into the den, had stimulated all that was in the pit into awareness and movement.

These eastern diamondbacks were just coming out of six months hibernation. Some were only three feet long, but then again, some were six feet and over. This was an unusual batch of many pit vipers, the deadliest poisonous snakes in North America. As it was, Fitz landed on top of multitudes of snakes, rolled over and over into them, unavoidably moved limbs under them, and—twisting and turning to extract himself—had snakes, little ones and big ones, all alive, all over him, a moving mass, around, above, and beneath. There were snakes, snakes, and more snakes.

Fitz was now experiencing the greatest possible horror—fear imaginable to him. Fitz heard the hissing, the rattling, and he could feel the snakes with his hands, on his face, and they were crawling under his shirt, on his belly, back, and neck, and up his pant legs. Again and again, they struck, sinking their poisonous fangs into this unwelcome intruder, the violator of their family's inner sanctum. No part of his body remained untouched, nor could he extricate himself from the many fangs penetrating his flesh. Fitz's screams were unheard by human ears nor would any know what had happened to him. His adrenaline and fear kept him conscious, even with the deadly venom filling all parts of his body, including his face and neck, swelling him to portions of ghastly rapidly decaying bodily decomposition. It was minutes before he blacked out. Fitz would return to consciousness, again and again, only to reexperience his terror over and over, until at last, he would expire.

As Rot stood looking into the pit, he was aware of the Silver and others of his mother's pack who stood with him. It began to rain, a light drizzle. In the mist materializing above the pit, Rot saw two red dogs staring into the pit, both belonging to his family of wolves. They were only there for a minute, and then they turned with eyes reflecting green beams of brilliant light. They looked at Rot, then swinging upward, they loped slowly at first and, with increasing speed, faded into the heavens, out of sight.

Preacher found Rot lying under the wagon wheel, leaning against the old gray barn. Somehow, he knew Rot would be there.

Rot heard him coming, and his nose told him who it was. The great dog rendered a few nostalgic whimpers—sounds of inner delight and satisfaction. Preacher said, "I knew you would be here. I have good news. Swift Hawk is still alive. He only had a slight wound and is recovered. All is well! Come on, boy! We're going home."[5]

---

[5] Timber rattlesnakes, eastern diamondbacks, begin to hibernate in October and emerge from hibernation at the end of April or early May. Pennsylvania boasts of some of the largest numbers of these snakes. A timber snake can have as many as eight to twelve babies at a time and will typically use the same den for hibernation their entire lives, which can span thirty or more years. Some eastern diamondbacks grow to over six feet in length. It is not unusual for a den of snakes to number above sixty or more snakes in them. Snakes returning to their den of origin in October are joined with many other members of their family in the same den.

About the Author

R. C. Besteder is from a small town called Kunkle, near Dallas in Northeastern Pennsylvania. He is a graduate of two colleges and holds three graduate degrees. R. C. served as a pastor of six churches over the course of twenty-one years and was a chaplain in the USAF for twenty-one years as well, retiring as a lieutenant colonel. He is the author of three books: *A Paradigm for Marital Intimacy*, in fulfillment of a doctor of ministry degree at Fuller Theological Seminary, Pasadena California; *Adam: You Are Descended from Adam! What About Adam*?; and *Red, The Saga of Red Dog*.

Besteder and his wife, Elaine, from Starke, Florida, have two children and one grandson. R. C. and Elaine live in DeLand, Florida.